STACK BEFORE YOU SPLURGE

A. ROY MILLIGAN

Lock Down Publications
Po Box 944
Stockbridge, Ga 30281

Visit our website @
www.lockdownpublications.com

Lock Down Publications
Like our page on Facebook: Lock Down Publications @
www.facebook.com/lockdownpublications.ldp

Stay Connected with Us!

Text **LOCKDOWN** to 22828 to stay up-to-date with new releases, sneak peaks, contests and more…
Thank you.

Submission Guideline.

Submit the first three chapters of your completed manuscript to ldpsubmissions@gmail.com, subject line: Your book's title. The manuscript must be in a .doc file and sent as an attachment. Document should be in Times New Roman, double spaced and in size 12 font. Also, provide your synopsis and full contact information. If sending multiple submissions, they must each be in a separate email.

Have a story but no way to send it electronically? You can still submit to LDP/Ca$h Presents. Send in the first three chapters, written or typed, of your completed manuscript to:

LDP: Submissions Dept Po Box
944
Stockbridge, Ga 30281

DO NOT send original manuscript. Must be a duplicate. Provide

your synopsis and a cover letter containing your full contact information.

Thanks for considering LDP and Ca$h Presents.

CONTENTS

I want to dedicate this book to my mom, RIP. Love you and thank you for everything…

CHAPTER ONE

Omies rolled over in his bed knocking three ounces of crack to the floor from his nightstand. Still, he was able to turn off the obnoxiously loud alarm clock that had been ringing for the last couple of minutes. It was seven in the morning and Sasha was busy down below his waist, slobbering all over his manhood. She had been awake for about an hour and a half and was beginning to get bored sitting up by herself, so she figured she would wake up Omies with a morning surprise. It had been five years now since her and Omies had met and so far, they couldn't get enough of each other in between the sheets.

Sasha was 23, mixed with Mexican, German, and black. She had long, beautiful, black hair, high cheekbones that lit up whenever she laughed. She had startling, blue-green eyes, and stood about 5'6" with an athletic frame.

She had a body to die for. Her big, round titties bounced in a way that only natural ones would. Omies on the other hand, was 22 and towered over Sasha at 6'1". He was bi-racial, mixed with black and white. His facial hair was full, and he kept it trimmed to perfection. The hair was clipped close to his face, lined up and he sported 360 waves. Together the two of them could have graced the pages of Jet magazine. Sasha gripped his hard dick with her soft, warm hands and with a slow rhythm, inserted his length down her throat as far as she could. Gagging wasn't an option anymore, she had been sucking, and deep throating his nine inches for years now and she knew exactly how to get him off. She ran her hands up and down his saliva coated dick in slow motion as she sucked hard then soft causing his dick to slightly jump.

Omies was lying back, enjoying every second of Sasha's hot mouth and twirling tongue. Glancing up, Sasha noticed that Omies eyes were rolling in the back of his head when she started using her tongue to tease his balls, while still not missing a beat as she stroked him with her hand. Minutes later, Omies body begin to jerk. She licked her way back to the top and gripped the pulsating head of his dick with her soft lips and began sucking aggressively until she felt the warm drops of fluid fill her mouth. Sasha greedily swallowed every drop he had to give her until he was drained.

"Baby, I'm ready. Get up!" Sasha said in a soft voice, while wiping her face and lips. Her class started at 8:00am and she hated being late, but since she didn't have a car of her own anymore, she had to operate on Omies schedule. It wasn't that big of a deal, because he didn't have a regular nine to five job nor was he looking for one, but he made sure she was at her class and her job every day. She had much love and respect for him because of that. So far, work and school were all her life consisted of. She would be gone all day, from morning until about 10:00 at night.

CHAPTER TWO

After stretching his arms and legs out, Omies got up and put on the same clothes he had on yesterday. He washed his face and brushed his teeth, weighed out a quarter ounce of crack on his digital scale then headed out the door, right behind Sasha.

"You have to drive, I don't feel good. I think I have a hang-over or something," Omies complained, rubbing the side of his temples.

"Okay, that's fine, I'll drive. You want me to stop at the gas station and get you something?" She asked, getting behind the wheel of his new black BMW 760 on chrome rims.

"Yeah, please." Omies said, as he got inside, wincing as the sound of the door shutting hurt his head. He leaned his seat all the way back and and began to relax as Sasha started to drive. Soon his phone was ringing.

"Hello."

"Hey what's up dude? Where can I meet you?" Judy asked.

"Damn Judy! What you doing up this early?" Omies said already wishing he didn't answer the phone. "I got a lot of things to do today, lots of running around. My daughter got into some crazy ass shit last night, so I have to bail her out of jail. My son needs a jump on his car, and my husband is driving me crazy, asking me to do shit for him! So now I'm on the go! I figured if I start early, I'll be able to get all of this stuff done, ya know?"

"Yeah, I feel you on that. Meet me at the University in Auburn Hills, in the parking lot, right by the security office," Omies said.

Right away Judy went off, "Security office? Why the Security office? I ain't going by no security, have you lost your damn mind?!"

"Look, it's cool. That's where I'm meeting someone else and I'm not about to be running all over the world this morning."

"Okay, if you say it's straight, that'll do. Why you sound like you straining to talk? Are you on the toilet Omies? You're gross!" Judy asked, sounding grossed out.

Omies hated talking on the phone to Judy. She talked too much and asked way too many questions. She was full of energy.

He didn't want to talk to her anymore, so without answering her question, he passed the phone to Sasha, while she was driving.

CHAPTER THREE

"Who is it?" she whispered before talking on the phone.

"Judy crazy ass," Omies said as he sat the phone on her lap and leaned back into the seat. He knew Sasha didn't want to talk to her either, but he wasn't giving her any choice today.

Rolling her eyes she grabbed the phone, "Hello!"

"Hey girl! I don't know what's wrong with O, you two fighting or something?" Judy asked.

"Nah, we ain't fighting, he sick right now, he not feeling well at all."

"Oh, I was wondering. He was sounding pretty grumpy on the phone. Is he going to be okay? You know they got that bird flu thing going around? You should probably take him to emergency if it's that bad. Do you know what's wrong with him?"

Sasha smiled the whole time as she listened to Judy ramble on. She ignored everything Judy had asked and instead said, "He wants you to meet him at the University, in the parking lot, next to where the Security office is located. We should be there in about twenty minutes, so be there please, because I have to be to class soon."

"Okay honey," Judy said now rushing to get off the phone.

"Bye!" Sasha said as she gave the phone back to Omies. "That lady is crazy! She just be talking about nothing no matter if you're talking back or not."

"Who you telling? Remember the last time we met up with her? When I got inside her car to get the money, she just started on about how her kids and old man got her into so much debt. I was in the car for like forty minutes. After I realized she wasn't about to stop talking, I had to lie to get out of there."

Sasha started laughing, "You still want me to stop at the gas station?"

"Yeah, why not. You got time, right?" Omies asked, making sure she was on time.

"I'll be on time."

Soon they arrived at the gas station. "You want something to take into class with you?" he asked, opening his door halfway.

"Yeah, get me an apple donut and orange juice please," Sasha said.

"An apple donut? Where they be at?"

"They right there in the front, with all the other donuts," she said, pointing him towards the cashier area.

"Oh, okay, I got you."Minutes they arrived at the University parking lot and parked next to a white security truck. There was a dark-skinned guy behind the wheel, waiting for Omies to get in. This was one of Omies' regular customers. He got out, leaving Sasha inside while she ate her donuts.

Sasha didn't like that Omies sold drugs, but she was so in love with him she accepted it. She also knew he messed around with other females, but she looked passed that as well. As long as he kept it away from her, she was willing to look the other way.

"What's up Sherman? You alright?" Omies asked.

"Naw, not really! Things have been crazy man," Sherman said as sweat dripped from his face.

Looking around like this was a set-up, Omies asked, "What's wrong? Why you shaking and sweating so fucking much?"

"I just got done arguing with my fucking wife. She brought her trifling ass up to my job, tripping over some number she found in my pants pocket. She's threatening me about taking my kids away and she's going to leave me," Sherman said, explaining what was going on.

"Y'all was fighting or something?"

"It started as just arguing, then it turned into a wrestling match. She took my wallet and told me I wasn't leaving, and I was trying to get it back from her..." Sherman said as tears started to fall from his eyes. "I know she's done this time. She going to leave my ass, I know it, I can feel it," he sobbed out, wiping the tears on his uniform sleeve. Omies was just sitting there listening and looking around.

"Sorry, I didn't mean to bring you into this," Sherman said, drying his tears.

"It's cool man, here's this." Omies said as he was getting ready to hand him the crack. Then he paused. "You got the money?"

"Naw man! That's what I've been saying, she took everything I had!" he shouted, still shaking.

Omies didn't believe him for one second. "Well you gonna have to call me when you get it. You already in the hole," he said cutting the conversation short.

"Come on O', you know I get my check next week."

"I can't do it right now."

"Well break me off a little piece so I can get my smoke on."

"I can't do it right now, call me when you got the money. Don't forget you already owe me out of that check you get next week," he reminded him.

"I know, I got you man! When have I ever played you?"

"Played me? Just now, having me drive all the way here and you aint got no money. Shit, you just played me last week too nigga! I met up with you and you gave me some story about getting robbed. I'm not about to keep giving you my shit! Don't call me until you get my money! I'm tired of you putting me on these dry ass runs! Whatha' fuck you think, I just like riding around with dope on me and shit!"

CHAPTER FOUR

"o you can't help me out, brother?" Sherman asked, clearly not getting it.

"Naw, man! I'm out, hit me up when you got some money!" Omies said as he began to get out of the truck.

Sasha was sitting patiently and relaxing until she noticed Omies staggering around, bleeding and panicking as he gasped for air.

"Oh my God! Omies, what happened?" Sasha screamed as she got out of the car to guide him inside. She didn't know what to do. The sight of so much blood had her frozen and unable to move or respond.

"Get…out…of here!" Omies said, barely able to talk. "He…stabbed me. Go…Go to the hospital. Arrghh, shit!!!" he managed to push out of his lungs.

"Okay, okay baby! Just relax and breathe! Don't stop breathing, you hear me! I'm gonna get you to a hospital! Oh shit!" she shouted, putting the car in drive, and out of nowhere Sherman jumped on the hood of the car, holding a big knife and demanding her to stop the car and unlock the doors. He looked like a crazed animal and scared her so much she couldn't even utter a single word. His blood shot eyes were bulging out of his head.

"Bitch, unlock the door!" Sherman was beating on the windshield so hard his face and hands were turning purple. He was pouring sweat and it didn't even look like the Mr. Sherman who said hi to her in the parking lot every day. She had never seen him like this or imagined he could be so dangerous. She knew he smoked a little crack and shot heroin from time to time, but she had never seen him go nuts over it. As she stared into his eyes, she started backing the car up until he fell off. Heading towards the exit, she passed Judy up, who was trying to flag them down, but she was busy trying to save Omies life. Blood was staining the entire chest of his shirt and she couldn't tell where he had been stabbed or how bad it was.

"Oh my God Omies, please don't die baby! Please don't die!" She cried out, while weaving in and out of traffic like she was a Nascar driver. Omies sat slouched in the passenger seat, on the verge of blacking out from all the blood he was losing.

"Just hold on baby! We almost there," Sasha promised, still weaving through the morning rush hour traffic. She was speeding, going at least 80mph.

Finally, she had to stop at a red light because the car in front of her stopped. While she was waiting for the light to turn green, she remembered that Omies could still have drugs on him. She knew that once he got to the hospital, they would be ripping and cutting his clothes off in an attempt to find all of the stab wounds and would most likely be nosey about the contents of his pockets. She reached over and searched his pockets. Luckily, the first one she searched held the dope inside. It was one big chunk of crack and she noticed her hand was trembling as she held it. Knowing she had to think fast. When the light turned green, Sasha smashed the pedal to the floor tailgating the car in front of her until it moved over. Speeding up, Sasha passed the car that had just switched lanes and noticed a little old lady driving. "Oops, sorry," Sasha said, feeling bad until she saw the old lady throw up her middle finger.

In the midst of driving to the hospital, she was still racking her brain trying to figure out what to do with the crack she had just pulled out of Omies pocket. She soon threw it out the window and kept driving.

Minutes later, she arrived at the hospital, trying desperately to save the love of her life. She didn't want to lose him. She knew she was number one in his eyes and he always made sure she had everything she needed. By the time the nurse had come out with a stretcher to get Omies, he had blacked out. He was still leaking blood when they put him on the stretcher and rolled him inside. He looked so helpless lying there, but luckily it wasn't as bad as either of them thought.

CHAPTER FIVE

Kareem stood out in most crowds at 6'4" tall and weighing in at 200 plus pounds. Slim was a full foot shorter, but he was also skinny as hell. So skinny, everyone just called him Slim. Sometimes they called him Big Bird too because he was high yellow. Kareem was the opposite in every way. Dark, thick mustache and a Rick Ross beard. Although he was a big guy, he kept himself up pretty well. He always wore a snap back when he was away from home, but underneath was a bald head. Slim had been over for a few hours and they were playing Madden for money.

"What up with them muthafuckas that just moved over here a couple months ago?" Slim asked.

"Who? There's a lot of people that move in and out of here all the time." Kareem responded.

"Them two dudes. One is Mexican or rican and the other one is black or Rican."

"Oh them? I don't know yet, but I think them niggas pushing some heavy weight, especially the black one. I don't ever see him gone for more than a few hours at a time, so I know he aint got no job, but yet he still pushing a new Beamer."

"I know I peeped that too. One night I saw him come home on the late night tip with a white bitch. I was about to rob him then, until his homeboy drove up right after him. That night, God was with him and her, because they were both about to get it," Slim said with a devilish grin on his face while continuing to beat Kareem at Football.

"The Rican dude drove up?"

Kareem asked, trying to keep up with the conversation and the game.

"Yup! He was with a female too. I coulda' got them both, but I gave them a pass."

Kareem laughed, "What you do, get scared nigga?"

"Hell naw! I'm just trying to be cautious. It's only about twelve black folks in this entire complex. I ain't

about to let one of these white folks call the police on me. So like I said nigga, I was being cautious."

Kareem looked at him sideways and laughed again. "You silly boy, but yeah, them nigga's roommates. They always got females and shit over there. I never see other dudes there. I think the Rican dude has a job though. I don't even know if he hustles or not. If he do, he's fooling me because I don't ever see him with fresh clothes and kick's on," Kareem said, finally scoring a touchdown on a flea-flicker play.

"That don't mean shit! He probably trying to be lowkey."

"Lowkey? Look at his damn roommate, that nigga' couldn't be lowkey if he wanted to!"

"Trust me, both them nigga's hustling, unless them nigga's people got money. I know I aint about to stay with a nigga' that's hustling and I'm not. Why the fuck I'ma put myself in the middle of all that bullshit that comes with that for?"

"Yeah, you got a point with that. Well I'ma find out soon enough, believe that," Kareem promised Slim with a serious expression on his face.

Kareem was only 25 years old and he had already done a five year stretch in prison for a drug case. He was finally running low on the money he had been living off, which was $200,000 he had robbed and killed an old friend for. The last few months he had been rounding up money to pay his rent.

Slim was a year older than Kareem and an ex-drug dealer as well. They both went from selling drugs to everyone in their neighborhood to robbing everyone in their neighborhoods. They had both been shot numerous times, but since they had to eat, there was no stopping them. Now, Omies and Carlos had just made it on their hit list.

It was almost 8:00 p.m. and the sun was going down. "I know you ain't forgot about what we was supposed to do today."

"Hell naw, I ain't forgot. I was thinking to wait until at least 10:00 tonight," Kareem said, trying to make sure it was perfect.

"Man, fuck that!" Slim said, throwing his controller to the floor. "Let's go get that nigga right now! You know he just re-upped today! We need to catch him now, while he got that bag!"

"Well, text Resa and see if she still at his crib. See what's up real quick, because I'm not moving until Resa give us the word. The last time you was rushing. We left early and we had to wait like two hours." Kareem said, reminding Slim of his previous fuck-ups.

"Man, that wasn't even my fault! That was your sister who was bullshitting."

"Just call her, or text her and see what's up."

Slim texted Resa right away and minutes later, Resa hit him up, saying that they were about to have sex. That made Slim mad because ever since he has known Kareem, he was trying to get with one of his sisters. They didn't give him any play because he was Kareem's friend.

"Nigga, it's time right now! They in the sheets, suit up!"

CHAPTER SIX

As soon as Kareem heard that, he went straight to his room and put on his black pants, black hoodie and his black steel toed boots. Five minutes later, they were both walking out the door with two pistols a piece, fully loaded. Slim had a pair of matte black, 9mm Glocks and Kareem had two black, 40 cal's. On their way to the car, they spotted Omies roommate, Carlos. He was stepping out of his dark blue mustang and he had a light skinned girl with him.

"There go that Rican muthafucka right there! I should run up on that nigga right now." Slim said pulling out his piece and cocking it.

"Naw, just chill dog! We gonna get them both. Just be patient." Kareem said, tugging on his arm. We got other business right now and I don't want to leave Resa there too long!"

"Man he can't even see me! Let me run up on him and strip him real quick," Slim asked, salivating at the mouth like a chained dog waiting for a chance to attack.

"Naw, nigga' that's gonna mess everything up. Chill!" Kareem said grabbing the back of his sweater. More forcibly this time. "If you get him right now for a couple thousands that's in his pockets, what if that cause him to move tomorrow? Then we can't get the bigger piece of the pie. Think big, you petty ass nigga." Kareem said.

"Fuck you! I am thinking big!" Slim said as he followed behind him, still talking shit under his breath.

"Whatever! That would have been dumb as hell if you woulda ran up on him for what's in his pockets."

Slim sat quietly not really knowing what to say. He knew Kareem was right, but he hated to pass up money. There was nothing Slim could do about it. He wasn't about to make a move without his boy by his side.

Soon they were close to the destination. They coasted down the last few houses with their lights off. It was dark, but the tall pole lights that were on every front yard, lit up the area more than they would have liked. Anyone looking out their window would see them creeping up the road. Kareem pulled the car over to the side and they noticed that the whole house they were setting up was dark inside, and Dayshawn's black Navigator was sitting in the driveway. Dayshawn was a pretty big drug dealer around the city of Southfield and Kareem had been plotting on him for about five months now. He put his sister on the inside so she could get close to him and it took her months to get close enough to spend the night. Tonight was like her seventh time spending the night with him and she was sick of him and his small dick. She had been keeping her eye on him and his money, getting his scheduled pick-ups and deliveries. Everything she saw or heard, she reported back to her brother.

Outside the front door, Kareem counted to three softly and then they creeped through the front door. Resa had left it unlocked for them while Dayshawn was in the shower. They crept right through, not making a sound. They could hear Resa's loud moans coming from the door. She was playing her part to perfection, it sounded like she was getting rammed hard. Approaching the bedroom door, they cocked their pistols and edge closer to the door. The moans became louder and louder and it sounded like Resa was getting fucked in the ass from the words that was coming from her mouth. Just hearing her making those sounds was making them both mad. Slim was mad because he was wishing he was the one fucking her.

CHAPTER SEVEN

Sasha left the hospital with Omies after he had his neck stitched and patched up. What they both thought was really bad turned out to be fine. He lost some blood, but overall, he was fine. He ended up with stitches in his neck and more in his chest. The ride home was quiet because Omies was asleep from the pain pills he had been given. Not only had Sasha missed school, but work as well, but she called into both and covered herself.

She soon pulled up to the burger joint and got a burger, fries and then ordered the same for Omies in case he woke up and was hungry.

While ordering the food from the drive-thru, she noticed Omies phone was vibrating. It had been ringing all day, so she put it on vibrate to not disturb Omies. This time the same person was calling back to back. Sasha answered his phone earlier at the hospital, but that was when Omies was awake. She was nervous about answering it now that he was sleep, she knew how mad he would get. Carlos had called earlier, and she answered it then told him what had happened. Carlos was shocked but told her that he would handle all of Omies business today. A few months ago, Carlos and Omies had discovered that they were good friends. In the past they were just competitors in the same city selling drugs. Today, they were roommates and got along really well. Realizing they had a lot in common, besides just the love of making fast money. The only thing Carlos didn't like about Omies, was that he was too damn flashy. The way he dressed, the jewelry he wore and even the BMW he drove, was way too much and it attracted unwanted attention from the police, and attention from the niggas who loved to rob. Everywhere he went people either thought he was a drug dealer or a rapper. Even though the car wasn't in his name, it still painted a target on his back because people saw him driving it every day. It was crystal clear that the car was for Omies, no matter whose name it was in. The whole ride back to Omies place his phone was being blown up and Sasha was beyond mad! She couldn't believe that some girl named Hillary kept calling him for more than an hour straight.

Who the fuck is this bitch and how come she feel like she can call my man all the time, Sasha thought to herself. She never bothered confronting him about her. She wanted to answer the phone so bad, but instead she threw the phone at Omies chest, right where they stitched him at, waking him out of his sleep. "Wake up, we home!" Sasha shouted with an attitude. She had been reading his text messages all day.

"Ow, damn baby! Why you throwing shit at me? You know I just got stitched up," Omies said, opening his eyes.

Sasha ignored him and got out the car and slammed the door shut. Out of nowhere another woman's voice started yelling, "Bitch, what you doing driving Omies car? And where the hell is he?"

Sasha looked around, but it was too dark to really see anyone or where the voice was coming from. *Who the fuck is that?* Sasha asked herself and when she turned back around, a brown skin girl was coming towards her with no shoes on.

"Bitch, who the fuck is you? You better hope you a cousin or sister driving my nigga's shit!" Hillary spat, now up close in Sasha's face. Omies was stumbling out the car when he saw Sasha smack Hillary across the face with the restaurant bag she had been holding. Fries and burgers went all over the place.

"Hold on, chill the fuck out!" Omies shouted as he tried his best to break the girls up and push them apart. They were going blow for blow with each other. It was hard for

Omies to break them up because they were swinging so wild and when he got in between he ended up getting hit. He was still weak from the loss of blood, the pain medication and antibiotic pills that the hospital had given him, so there was no breaking up anything for him. It didn't take him long to realize he didn't have the energy to stop the fight, so he backed off and let them continue on. The girls were surprisingly still on their feet, but 5 seconds later, Hillary knocked Sasha to the ground, but that didn't stop anything. She got up and they were both still swinging away. Omies just shook his head, picked up the car keys from the ground and walked inside the apartment, leaving them both outside. Sooner or later someone was going to call the police on them. There was nothing he could do besides yell at them to stop, but they weren't trying to hear none of that. The whole scene was so loud that curtains were being pulled back. Someone was bound to think a woman was getting attacked.

As soon as Omies walked inside, he saw Carlos sitting on their navy-blue couch, with cream lining. He was having a drink with a pretty female that Omies had never seen before. *Damn*, he thought to himself as he looked her up and down like a piece of choice meat. "What's up?" Omies asked, as he closed and locked the door behind him.

"What's up with you fool? You alright? You out there getting careless and getting stabbed and shit, what's up with that? You ready to take care of that muthafucka or what?" Carlos asked.

"Yeah, you know that's in motion already. That nigga probably would have killed me if he coulda, but I wasn't careless, just dealing with the wrong person. I'm good though," Omies said, not wanting to say too much more in front of the new girl.

Carlos took the hint and just laughed everything off. "Well I'm glad he didn't kill you, rent about to come up soon. I need that $850 out your back," Carlos joked and they all started laughing.

"I know it's none of my business, but is that $850 a piece, or is that the whole rent?" The sweet thang asked, looking embarrassed for even asking.

"Naw sweetheart, it's $1700 a month to live in one of these." Omies said as he sat down on the couch next to her. "Who's your friend? You not going to introduce us?" Omies asked.

"Calm down, I was going to after we was done talking. This my baby, Olivia. Olivia, this my roommate, Omies,"

"Nice to meet you." Olivia said softly and smiled.

"Nice to meet you too. Where you from? I ain't never seen you before. You have a sister, twin, or cousin that look like you for me? I need a girl." Omies said.

Olivia laughed, but before she could answer his question, they all heard a loud bang at the door. Carlos grabbed his piece from underneath the couch cushion and asked, "Who the fuck is that?"

"Chill man! Just chill out! That's just Sasha and Hillary crazy ass," Omies said going to the door.

"You sure man?" Carlos asked paranoid because he knew there was still dope in the house. "Yeah, they was just outside fighting. Listen, you can hear their voice from here." Omies said as he held up his hand to quiet Carlos and sure enough you could hear both voices cursing up a storm.

"Well, go get them hoes before the neighbors call the cops. Damn, why you didn't say nothing earlier? You know we got shit all over this house nigga." Carlos said reminding him.

"Nigga, they tripping out there. I tried to stop them, but I can't do nothing to them right now. I'm doped up and weak as hell. You go out there and stop them, bad ass," Omies said, challenging Carlos to do it.

"Well it sounds like they done now," Carlos said, noticing the blood on Omies's face. Smirking, he just shook his head and laughed. 'They probably just wanna talk now and dog your ass, open it up," Carlos said, daring Omies to open the door.

Carlos knew that was bringing to much heat, and he wasn't trying to deal with any police. The girls banged and screamed at the door for a few more seconds, then they started kicking the door, like they were the police.

"Aw hell naw! These bitches tripping!" Omies said, yanking the door open and grabbing them both by their hair, slamming them to the floor like rag dolls. He then stood over them. "Y'all better shut the fuck up, I got neighbors." he demanded.

"Fuck you nigga! Nigga you ain't shit! Who the fuck is this bitch?" Sasha shouted trying to kick him.

"Bitch? Bitch, you a bitch!" Hillary yelled back at her.

"Hey! Hey! Hell naw, y'all gotta chill the fuck out in here! Y'all got shit fucked up! Now y'all disrespecting me," Carlos yelled, getting red in the face.

"I'm sorry Carlos," Sasha said as she stormed to the back of the apartment to Omies room to pack her things. Both girls looked tired with dirt and grass stains all over their clothes. Their faces and arms were all scratched up like they had been rolling in a bunch of rose bushes. "So you wasn't gonna tell me about her?" Hillary asked, getting in his face.

"Man, I been told you I had a girl! You know, I don't even fuck wit you like that," Omies told her, pushing her outta his face.

"Since when don't you answer your phone all fucking day when I call?" Hillary asked to know, jumping back in front of him.

"Hillary look... I got a girl," Omies tried to explain, but she cut him off.

"Bitch, she's not your girl! She just the main bitch your sorry ass fuck with, so once again, why the fuck you couldn't answer your damn phone all day for me Omies?"

"Because I was in the hospital! Damn! Somebody tried to rob me today! If you calm your hyper-ass down and find out what's going on before you start swinging, we'll be alright. You see this shit? He cut my neck all up. If I hadn't seen it coming, I'd probably be dead right now! Luckily I was able to fight back, but he still got me pretty good," Omies said, laying it out for her.

CHAPTER EIGHT

As she listened to every word that was coming out his mouth, she began to view the bandages on his neck and the hospital wristband around his wrist. She was starting to feel silly for snapping like she did. Tears started to creep from her eyes as she began to apologize.

"I'm so sorry O'. I didn't know, I swear, I didn't know. I feel so stupid now." Hillary said, eyes full of tears that began to fall down her cheek bones.

Omies grabbed her and hugged her. He felt she was sincere and speaking from the heart and said, "It's okay boo, stop crying."

She couldn't stop crying, so she squeezed him even tighter, "Please forgive me," Hillary pleaded with him.

"It's cool boo, now stop crying. Just know that you got some serious making up to do," Omies joked, still holding her in his arms.

Hillary giggled, which blew snot out of her nose on accident and onto his shirt, but still the tears fell. "Omies, I am so sorry," she said, still crying but not as hard.

"Okay, chill for a minute, I'll be right back," he said before heading to his room to check on Sasha.

Carlos and Olivia just sat there during the whole thing, listening to what was going on like they were watching an episode of love and hip hop.

When Omies walked into his room, Sasha had a pink Piston's duffel bag packed and she was ready to go. She only had two drawers of her own, so it didn't take her long to get everything into one bag. She was upset with Omies because he put her through too much bullshit and thought that it was okay. Since day one she had never gotten into a physical fight with a girl over Omies, so she knew in her own mind that him and Hillary was serious for her to act like that.

Sasha stormed out of the room as she seen Omies face. She pushed him out of her way, not even trying to hear him. She yanked the door open, ignoring Hillary who was still in the living room like she lived there and walked out to the parking lot and got into the car with her mother, who she called from the bedroom. Omies knew she was mad at him because she had never called her mom to come get her. Usually she would just make him take her home. Omies felt bad because of all the marks that were on her face. He couldn't even tell who had won, because they both had scratches.

Slim kicked in the bedroom door with his size twelve, Timberland boot and pointed his guns, while Kareem followed behind him holding his two guns "POLICE, FREEZE! PUT YOUR FUCKIN' HANDS UP!" They yelled rushing into the room like they was real SWAT team members.

Dayshawn and Resa were butt ass naked in the doggie style position. Resa began screaming, as she grabbed ahold of Dayshawn, that is until Slim snatched her by her hair, and pointed the gun at her head and said, "Bitch shut the fuck up before I break you're fuckin' jaw," Slim demanded while he eyed her naked body. Her skin looked so soft and he noticed she was perfectly shaved.

Resa quieted down real quick at the sight of the guns. She looked vulnerable with her naked body shivering and then she started crying, playing her role to the fullest like she was after an Academy Award. This wasn't the first guy she went out with for months or even years and then later set them up to get robbed for thousands of dollars.

Kareem was busy tossing Dayshawn all over the room. Slinging his light ass into the mirror mounted behind his dresser and then pistol whipping him a few times. He wasn't trying to knock him out completely, he just wanted it to be known that they wasn't playing no games. Resa was in the center of the bed, while Dayshawn had his head put through the wall and then had a lamp smashed over his bleeding head.

"Where da cash at nigga!" Kareem pointed the pistol in his face.

"Come on man, that's what this about?" Dayshawn said with blood dripping out of his mouth, nose, and scalp.

Kareem hit him in the forehead with the butt of the gun, sending him to his knees, and then mashing him face first into the floor, "What the fuck you mean? Yeah, this about the money bitch ass nigga! Cough that shit up my nigga," Kareem said, kneeling down on the bloody, shag carpet and putting the gun in Dayshawn mouth until he started to gag.

Pulling his head away, Dayshawn said, "Alright man, it's in the closet! Hold on, just chill out! You can have it all man!" Dayshawn whined, letting them know he was tired of getting hit in the head. Kareem snatched him up and pushed him into the closet where a big safe was hiding behind some hanging clothes. This was a serious neat freak. All his clothes were labeled with each day of the week, even his socks were tightly rolled up and stacked neatly. Dayshawn couldn't be more than five and a half feet, and weighed less than 170 lbs. He was shaking and had already pissed all over himself.

"Open it!" Kareem ordered with a greedy grin on his face, but noticed Dayshawn was moving slow, like he was trying to prolong things in case someone heard the commotion and called the cops. "Hurry the fuck up!" Kareem yelled, hitting him across the face with his pistol breaking fresh skin off his cheek. Blood flowed down the side of his face, down his neck, and then chest.

CHAPTER NINE

"Alright, alright!" Dayshawn cried out, as he began to put the combination in, seconds later the safe popped open, revealing stacks of cash and a couple blocks of cocaine. The cocaine odor was so strong Kareem could smell it soon as he opened the safe.

"This is all I got dog!" Dayshawn whined, hoping they believed him.

Kareem smacked him on the forehead again with his gun, "Check underneath the mattress!" Kareem shouted, not believing this was all he had. "Nigga, you stay in a nice ass crib and be driving these nice cars with no job or business and you gonna tell me this all you got? Do I look stupid?" Kareem asked, hitting him again, this time splitting the back of his head open. Blood started pouring out, and Dayshawn began to feel woozy.

His vision was going in and out and he knew it wouldn't be long before he fainted if they kept hitting him. He could barely see or hear what they were saying.

"I swear man, that's all I got! I might have a couple dollars in my pants pocket over there on the floor, oh and some jewelry in the top drawer, but that's it!"

For some reason Kareem believed him and gave up on recovering anything else. He figured if he beat him any worse he'd end up killing him and he wasn't about to leave his sister there with a dead man.

"What you find?"

"Just some guns and some jewelry," Slim said, sitting on the bed next to Resa.

"Check them pants over there for me," Kareem said not at all cool with Slim pushing up on his sister.

Kareem gathered up the handguns and threw them in a pillowcase with the rest of the money. "Let's roll!" Kareem ordered, walking out the door. They left out the house the same way they came in, breaking the lock off as they exited. When they left Dayshawn was passed out and bleeding from several gashes on his head and face. They fucked him up good....

They drove back to kareem's place, looking in the rear-view mirror the whole time. Finally they arrived and put everything on the table and begin splitting. Dayshawn had the coke in separate baggies, which made it look like more than it was. When it was all weighed on the scale, it wasn't even a whole kilo.

"Did you see that bitch ass nigga?" Kareem asked mocking how Dayshawn was flopping around on the floor.

"Hell yeah!" Slim replied, laughing at Kareem, "That nigga really thought we was the police when we came in! He was frozed, I bet he did more than just piss his pants."

"Nigga, that was way easier than I thought it was gone be." Kareem said, nodding his head in agreement with Slim.

"I told you it would be, Dayshawn a bitch, he just playing a gansta. He's just hard to catch up with because he be moving from place to place. You know any nigga could get away like that." Slim said holding up a gold rope to the light to see what karat it was.

"Yeah, you right about that, I done hit a few nigga's coming out of the bars and clubs. Some of them, I threw in the trunk and took them to their crib to get the money."

"You know how I used to get down." Kareem said, rolling up a blunt.

"Yeah you be acting a fool on these nigga's!You think he had some more money in there?" Slim asked.

"Probably not there, but I believe he still got some more money and dope somewhere else. Why you ask that?"

"Because you was slapping the shit out of that nigga, I thought you was about to kill him."

"I told him to open the safe and shit and he just start moving slow as hell, so that's what made me hit his ass. He was playing games and shit like he was trying to stall or something. For a minute I thought he had an alarm and the police was gonna come."

"Unless he was trying to grab a gun or something? Look at all the guns we found underneath the mattress. You know he had to have more all over the house," Slim said, leaning back on the couch, enjoying his high.

"Yeah you right. He coulda been trying to grab a gun, but I think he knew better then to do that. I woulda splattered his ass all over that closet." Kareem bragged, grabbing a can of beer out of the fridge.

Resa was still in tears after her brother and Slim left. Although she knew everything was fake and set up on her behalf, she was still scared and that's what brought tears to her eyes. It was no joke having a gun pointed at your face. "Oh my God!" she cried while her hands was shaking out of control. "Dayshawn, Oh my God! What are you into? They could have killed us both and you didn't do shit," Resa accused him viciously.

Dayshawn was doing his best to sit himself up against the wall. "You okay?" he asked her, grabbing a towel and holding it to the back of his head, where the worst bleeding seemed to be coming from.

"Yes, I'm okay, but I'm scared. What if they come back? I don't want to sleep here tonight Dayshawn. You need to call the police," she said, trying to hold her tears back, while grabbing him another towel.

"Chill baby. Everything okay, them nigga's got what they wanted. They ain't coming back. Stop crying, everything gonna be okay." He assured her again, wondering if she remembered him whining and hollering like a little girl, then he thought again and said *"Fuck her,"* in his mind. *She ain't do nothing neither when they came in here.*

"Come on babe, get up. Sitting here crying ain't gonna help shit," Dayshawn told her getting pissed at her whining. He was the one bleeding, not her.

They stood up and Dayshawn looked under the bed and saw they had taken every single gun from under there. He walked back into the closet and grabbed an black pistol from underneath a hat and began walking around searching the house.

CHAPTER TEN

"**W**hat they take?" Resa asked.

"Just a little money. It ain't shit though, they only got some change."

He knew he was slipping big time, because he had never been robbed for this much money. Walking around the house with only boxers on and the gun in his hand, the only thing on his mind was selling one of his houses tomorrow for $50,000 to his plug. He had been wanting to buy the house from Dayshawn last year when he first saw it, but Dayshawn wouldn't sell it. He had paid only $30,000 for it and it was a five bedroom, three bath house in a not so good neighborhood. He had fixed up the interior with new windows, doors, paint, carpet, kitchen cabinets, stainless steel refrigerator and dishwasher, and two Jacuzzi tubs. Outside he had the roof redone and paid for modern landscaping work to be done. After all the work was finished, he spent $20,000 on remodeling, which set the house value to $109,000 within only six months. Now he was going to sell it for $50,000 just to get back on his feet.

As Dayshawn was walking through the house, he was thinking to himself, Fuck! *I can't believe this shit! Who the fuck even know where I stay at? This some bullshit! No way I'm keeping that much money where I sleep again. That shit going to the bank next time or I'm burying it. I wonder if they got on to me by just riding through the neighborhood and just happened to see my Navigator in the driveway on big rims and they thought I had money. Hatin' ass nigga's, it's cool though. I'ma have $50,000 tomorrow and this is just gonna make me stunt even harder on these haters.*

Carlos had just finished his last shot of Patron when he looked over and saw Olivia drop her dress to her ankles. This was her first night over, but they had been out on a few dates. As Carlos watched her strip for him, he was a little shocked that she was ready to give him some pussy. He wasn't expecting it no time soon, but he wasn't about to tell her to pull her dress back up either. He could feel the liquor creeping up on him, so he got up and locked the bedroom door. He could still hear Omies out in the living room arguing with one of the girls.

"How you feeling sweetheart?" he asked Olivia, eyeing her body through the sexy peach, two-piece set.

"I'm hot baby! It's hot in here," she said before falling on top of the bed. Olivia laughed at her ungraceful fall. Carlos could hear in her voice that she was drunk off the liquor they had consumed, but to Carlos she still seemed like she knew what was going on.

"Baby, you okay?" he asked caressing her shoulders.

"Yes baby I'm fine! Just hot and a little dizzy," she claimed, while still lying face down on the red, silk sheets.

Carlos laughed, "Come here, papi will take care of you."
"Here I come baby," she said, crawling on all fours to where he was and then she straddled him, lying on his chest, looking into his chestnut brown eyes.

Carlos did his best to strip down to his boxers with her on top and soon revealed the body he had been working on every other day.

They began kissing and Carlos noticed how soft and juicy her lips were. She gave him warm tongue kisses for almost five minutes straight, making Carlos think they would never get to the sex part. She was a really good kisser and showed off different tricks with her seductress tongue she was using on him. It only served to make him more excited and anxious to have sex with her. He started easing her panties to her ankles with one hand then his feet and she unsnapped her see through lace bra herself, revealing perfect, round titties and rock hard nipples. Carlos took off his boxers while aggressively sucking her titties enough so she knew he wanted every bit of her.

"Yeeesss baby, ahh yes, Sshhitt! That feel good baby!" she whispered into his neck, while her lips and tongue were busy kissing him.

Carlos flipped her off him slowly and laid her flat on her back and began kissing her from her stomach to her toes. He felt her body tremble once he began kissing her inner thighs and then biting them gently with his lips. She shook even more when he blew cool air in between her thighs. Finally he was face to face with her pretty, pussy lips. He could see her wetness dripping out of her insides. He moved closer, sticking his tongue out and running it over her clit while spreading her lips apart with his two fingers.

CHAPTER ELEVEN

"Oohh baby! " She moaned, spreading her legs even wider, offering his hot probing tongue greater access.

His tongue was flickering and flapping as fast as butterfly wings and that was driving her crazy. She was trying to move away from his wicked tongue, but he held her legs and wouldn't let her move until he had made her cum, then he moved up her body to her neck and lips, giving her a taste of her own juices, which she accepted without hesitation.

Ready to reciprocate, she reached for his dick and realized he wasn't even hard yet, so she turned him over on his back and started sucking his dick fast and sloppy. He began to moan a little as she started stroking him up and down, then she would take it out, spit on it and then suck and lick it again. After a few seconds his dick was standing at attention.

Olivia climbed on top of him like he was a stallion and inserted his dick inside her. Carlos wanted to say something about the condoms in the drawer next to him, but he was too turned on and too caught up in the moment to stop her. He knew he should be wearing one and he was praying she didn't have an STD, after all, he didn't know her all that well but his dick didn't care and seconds later neither did he.

Olivia rode him like a pro for a few minutes and then got off and started sucking his dick again, as if she loved the taste of her own pussy. "Damn baby!" he whispered, trying not to be so loud. "That's what I'm talking about, suck that shit!"

As he was talking to her she continued to suck away like she was devouring a Tootsie pop. She stroked him up and down, and twisting her hand around his dick and balls repeatedly until he grabbed the back of her head and said, "I'm about to cum! Oh baby, shit!!" he moaned, barely controlling his body.

She stopped and climbed back on top and began riding him again. Carlos was on fire because she had taken him all the way to his tipping point then just stopped, she didn't even let him get his nut off, and now it felt like his dick had swelled up even more. But she refused to let him cum if she couldn't yet, "Hell naw, turn your ass over," he said, flipping her over off him. Olivia loved how rough he was being.

He entered her and began pumping away, trying to get that nut back he had just lost. He started talking dirty to her and smacking her ass while he stroked her in and out as fast as he could.

"Yes, baby! Yes!" Olivia shouted as she threw her ass back onto his dick matching him thrust for thrust. "Fuck me baby! Yeah fuck me good!" All you could hear was a clapping noise and a mushy, wet sound from her pussy.

Carlos continued to ram her non-stop, pumping in and out like a machine right and left swirling his dick inside her making sure there was not an inch of her pussy that went untouched. The faster he went, the louder her moans got. Minutes later she screamed as her pussy squirted all over his dick, but still he pounded away, trying to get his nut too.

After he came, they both collapsed to the bed, with him still inside her. It felt way too good to pull out. The sheet and pillows were soaked with both their fluids. They lay there breathing hard and then out of the blue both of them started laughing.

"What you laughing for?" he asked her in the middle of laughing himself.

"You laughed first, what you laughing for?" She countered back at him.

He laughed again, "I don't know, probably because we breathing so hard and we were moaning so loud and now we just quiet as hell."

She started laughing again, "You couldn't have said it any better. I'm laughing at the same damn thing, you think your friend heard us?" Olivia asked, feeling a little embarrassed.

"Without a doubt with your loud ass,"

"For real?" She asked again with a big smile on her face.

Almost on cue, there was a knock on the door, "Who is it?" Carlos asked.

"Damn nigga, what you doing in there killing her?" Omies asked, joking around.

Carlos started laughing again and so did Olivia. "Naw dog we good," Carlos said as he got up and started putting on his pants. "You straight baby?" he asked admiring her sexy body.

"Yeah, I'm fine now! Super fine in fact."

CHAPTER TWELVE

"Omies you are so full of shit!" Hillary yelled at him, still pissed off.

"Man chill. You tripping for no damn reason! You bet not ever pull no bullshit like that again!" Omies said, sipping some Henny.

"Well, answer your phone next time and everything will be cool," she said, folding her arms across her breasts.

"Who the hell is you, that you feel like I need to be answering my phone every time you call?" Omies asked her.

"Because you the only nigga' I'm fucking, sucking and swallowing." Hillary reminded him.

"But you already know you not the only girl I'm fucking, so chill that crazy shit out! I ain't with all that drama shit. You on some bullshit!"

"I ain't on shit! You on some bullshit! Matter of fact, I'm tired of this sideline shit. So what? I can't be your girl? I'm not good enough to be with you O'?" she asked, now all up in his face, looking for an answer. She was hurt inside and she felt unwanted. She was beginning to feel like he cared for Sasha way more then he cared for her.

She hated that he was nearly running behind Sasha when she was on her way out the door. Hillary couldn't recall one time he ever chased after her.

"Man, chill out!" Omies said as he grabbed her and hugged her after seeing the tears getting ready to fall from her eyes. "You know you my baby. When I heal up I'ma take you some where special so we can talk about everything and on where we stand. I told you I want you to have my baby, so stop tripping!" he told her, which only made Hillary cry even more.

"You never let me spend the night anymore, is it because of Sasha?" she asked, still feeling hurt inside and thinking he was playing her for a fool. Omies didn't answer that, he just held her tighter and kissed her. Hillary and Omies had been dealing with each other for about three years now. She was so in love with him although she knew she wasn't his first choice on most nights. He still had a lot of love for her. She would do anything for him, no matter what. She had no idea that Omies was messing around with another girl more serious than her. She knew it was possible, but to see it was just heartbreaking for her. Sasha was a very pretty girl so it really made her mad that she didn't know about her, or heard her name come out of Omies mouth.

Omies use to always tell her about different girls he was having sex with, but he never told her about Sasha.

Omies spent money on Hillary and Sasha. He also bought Hillary a car that she had been driving for about seven months now.

"Here, you have to get cleaned up, look at you. Stop trying to fight with me all the time," he said, as he looked at her from head to toe. Hillary was Mexican and Black, with long black hair. Omies loved girls with long hair and he seemed to always run into and attract exotic looking females that were mixed with different nationalities.

"I don't be fighting all the time," Hillary said through a pouty and busted lip.

"Look at your lip, all busted up. You don't even look pretty no more," Omies teased her, trying to make her laugh a little.

She did and couldn't help but smile. "It looks that bad? I did beat that bitch ass though!"

On his mind was Sasha and he needed to get rid of Hillary, he was tired of dealing with her. "Look, I need you to take care of something for me. I can't go out all doped up like this, so call this number. Her name Judy and she owes me a thousand dollars for her car note. Go collect that for me," he said as he dialed the number into her phone.

"When I pick it up what you want me to do, bring it back here tonight?" Hillary asked rubbing the inside of his leg, letting him know she didn't mind coming back.

"Naw, not tonight. The doc said I need to sleep. Go buy yourself something nice tomorrow and hold the rest for me."

"Okay, I'll just put it with the rest," she said as he hugged her and sent her on her errand.

Omies called Sasha as soon as he locked the door.

Sasha didn't answer the first three times he called, but he continued to dial away and eventually she answered.

"What Omies? Why are you calling my phone like you crazy?" She asked him, not really caring what he had to say.

"Damn baby…," he started to say before she cut him off.

"Baby nothing…fuck you!" She yelled through the phone so loud he had to pull his phone away from his ear. "You should see my face! You think I like fighting with your hood rat ass bitches?"

"No baby, I don't."

"Stop calling me baby! I'm not your baby Omies! If I was, you wouldn't have left me outside to fight that girl! You would have been a man and broke that shit up!" Sasha said, not giving into him at all.

"I couldn't, I was too weak! You know the nurse gave me all them pills and shit! Just listen to me Sasha, you are blowing this out of proportion. We need to talk, I'm on my way," he said, trying to bully his way past her weak defenses.

"No Omies, I'm done! This is ridiculous! I deserve way better than this," she said, beginning to cry.

"Sasha, just let me come over and explain. It ain't nothing like that. I don't want that hoe! I want you. I want to be with you. I'm sorry for what happened tonight. It will never ever happen again, I promise. Just let me come over and talk to you please."

"No Omies! You know how my mom is. She is going to trip. She already thinks you hit me and I was covering for you, saying some other girl did it. It's way too late anyways. She already mad that she had to come and get me."

"Sasha, you 23 years old and it's only 11:00 p.m. I'm on my way," he insisted.

"No Omies, because if she put me out, what am I going to do? I don't have a car or a place to stay!"

"I'll get you a place tomorrow, your own shit, fully furnished."

"Whatever Omies, just like that new car you were going to buy me," Sasha said, reminding him of other unfilled promises.

"Aw shit, now you doubting your man. I told you to save up and I was going to help you, but since you doubting me, I'ma just take care of everything tomorrow myself. I got you," Omies promised her again.

"Don't be trying to buy me back. I am not for sale! I am not one of them sluts you be banging."

Omies laughed, "I'm not baby, I'm just really, really sorry about what happened tonight! I'm on my way though okay? Get ready! I love you and I'll see you in a couple minutes," Omies told her.

Her last defenses crumbled when he said he loved her, "Okay, I love you too!" Sasha said, sighing on the other end of the phone.

Omies hung up with a smile on his face. He then went to the shoe box that was under his bed. It was full of money.

Counting out $7000 cash, he threw it on his bed. Then he left to pick up Sasha. He was going to do his best to make it up to her. He knew she was right, he should have done more to keep the situation under control tonight, instead of just walking away.

While driving, Omies realized he didn't want to lose Sasha. He had never given much thought to how deep his feelings were for her until she said she was done and walked away. Now he was willing to do anything to get her back.

CHAPTER THIRTEEN

A week later Carlos and Omies was at home sitting around talking when a package was delivered to their front door from California. This was a package they received once a week at numerous addresses. Carlos opened it and inside was a medium sized Teddy Bear. He walked around to the kitchen with the bear, as Omies trailed behind, happy and smiling like a kid in a candy store. It was around noon and the sun was shining through the windows into the apartment. Carlos started cutting the Teddy Bear up and pulled out a whole kilo of cocaine. It was wrapped in grease and enclosed within saran wrap. Setting the kilo on the scale, Omies made sure it was all there.

"Right on point, as always!" Omies thought to himself as the four digits flashed on his scale.

Carlos then grabbed a fresh box of baking soda from the refrigerator, while Omies grabbed the Pyrex, a pot to boil water in, a spoon and a pointy stick he had made from a metal clothes hanger.

Carlos began blindering five ounces of cocaine down to powder form. He then poured it all out into the Pyrex along with some baking powder. Then he mixed everything around with the hanger piece and let the concoction heat up a bit. He added a teaspoon of hot water from the boiling pot the Pyrex was in and began working his wrist like a pro, swirling the mixture round and round. After all his hard work, it finally came time for the magic that he added to his recipe, cool water was thrown into the Pyrex and he watched his potion turn into a rocky substance. He had three large chunks and now all he needed to do was wait for them to dry. To help hurry that process along, he set the crack on napkins. He cooked five ounces but with everything he added, he was able to come out with nearly nine ounces.

When he was done, he had a couple of sales he had to take care of who had already been waiting for hours, so he left out with four ounces, while Omies continued cooking, using the microwave. Carlos hated using the microwave, but Omies loved it. He was able to do the same thing Carlos could do on the stove, in a microwave. Sometimes Omies would end up with more grams than

Carlos when he used the microwave as opposed to the stove.

Carlos drove for about thirty minutes, passing several attractive girls he wanted to stop for, but he had way too much dope on him. What he had on him would get him fifteen years or more in prison. He kept driving until he arrived in Pontiac, on Third Street, with his boxers stuffed full. Soon he pulled up to a driveway that belonged to a customer in a newly remodeled, yellow house.

The weather was a mild 65 degrees out and there were kids racing their bikes up and down the street. As soon as he walked inside the house, he could see there were six other fiends there who wanted to buy some dope as well. They each had their paychecks on them, and they were ready to spend it all. Carlos looked around and noticed Bill standing in the hallway. Carlos had known him for a while now. Bill was a white guy, who did carpet and roof work. He made a lot of money, most of which came to Carlos. "What's up stranger? Where the hell you been all day man?" Bill asked, happy to see him. He had been waiting for hours and each time he called, Carlos would tell him he was on his way.

"My bad man, I had to take my son to get his shots and shit today."

"Ohh, that's what it was? I was wondering man. What's that you got there? I need six quarter ounces. How much you're going to charge me for that?" Bill asked, hoping to get a good deal, since he was buying so much."Same thing I always charge you. Do the math!" Carlos said.

"Come on man, I'm getting six of them," Bill said, like it would make any difference to Carlos.

"I gotta make money too. I don't care if you just get one. Eventually you'll get six. You should know that I'm in no rush to do anything. Just because you buying six don't mean I'm dropping my prices." Carlos said acting like he didn't care if he sold him a drop.

"Whatever man, here ya' go!" Bill said as he started counting out $1,500 to pay Carlos with.

"Okay, call me when you need me again. I got some good shit in right now," Carlos said, as he put the money in his pocket.

Carlos drove off to meet his next customer, which was about ten minutes away. As soon as he arrived on the street, he called her to come outside and she came running like an obedient dog. She was a skinny ass black woman with short hair. She was wearing some blue jean shorts that came to her thighs and had a dirty, tan t-shirt on with some white, dingy sandals.

"Hey baby!" she greeted him when she got in the car.

She was smiling from ear to ear, even though she was missing most of her teeth. Looking at her, Carlos thought back to when he was fifteen and he had just met her. She had a little more weight on her then and still had all her teeth. He was coming out of the store with a bag of chips when he seen her begging for change.

"You got a quarter?" she asked, holding her hand out in case he did.

Carlos picked up his bike and dug into his pocket. He gave her fifty cents and said, "Here, this is all the change I have!"

"You got some more money that ain't change sweetie?" she asked him, hoping he had more.

"Why?" he asked, getting ready to pedal off down the street.

"Now, wait sweetie! I got something for you, just hear me out for a minute," she said coming closer.

"What you got for me?" Carlos asked, curious.

"You want to go somewhere with me?" she asked him, rubbing her sweaty hands on her legs.

"Go somewhere? Where?"

"Around the corner, you ever been with a grown woman before baby?" she asked, lifting up her shirt and showing him a dirty, silver belly ring she had. Carlos looked around to see if he noticed anyone he knew. He didn't want to get caught talking to no crack head. But she was talking either sex or some head, both were right up his alley. At the time he had only been with two girls and they were his age. He watched a lot of movies and heard his uncles and dad talking about paying for sex and now here he was getting approached. He had no idea they weren't talking about crack head whores, he just thought any chick was suitable at the time.

"How much?" he asked, a little nervous.

"Well it depends, how much you got?" she asked, wanting to get as much as she could from him. She licked her lips, trying to look irresistible and sexy. Her hair was tied in a straight ponytail and fell down her back, where it swung from side to side.

"I wanna fuck, how much is that?" he asked, tired of beating around the bush.

"You tell me how much you got sugar and I'll tell you what you can get for that much," she said, not giving in until she knew what he had.

"I got twenty dollars. What can I get for that?"

"Okay, let's go! I live around the corner," she said, pointing down the street.

"Here, hop on. I'll give you a ride over there."

"You better not drop me boy!" she said as she got on the front of the bike's handle bars.

"Don't worry, I got you," he said, pedaling as fast as he could straight to where she lived. Out front, on the porch, was an old lady in a wheelchair that looked very old. It was her mother and she was disabled. Silvia was able to sneak Carlos past her and up to her room. While Silvia closed the door, Carlos could see there was nothing but a bed in the room. He turned around and got nervous when Silvia started stripping off her clothes, until she was butt naked, standing in front of him.

"You ready? I ain't got all day!"

Carlos could only nod his head up and down, he couldn't bring himself to speak.

"Okay, sit on the bed and I'll do all the work baby," Silvia said as she unbuckled his pants and pulled them down to his ankles. Then she pulled his shirt up and over his head and noticed he wasn't even hard. "Even though you didn't have enough money to pay for some head, I'ma do it for free until you get hard," she said, lowering her head into his lap.

Carlos heart was beating so fast, he swore she could hear it. He was speechless as her warm, wet mouth swallowed his dick. She began sucking for a few seconds, until he was hard and ready. Then she put a condom on him using only her mouth, a trick he had never seen or heard of before in his young, fifteen years of living.

She rode his dick for less than five minutes before Carlos busted a nut and was ready to get out of there. He gave her the twenty dollars and clearly ran out the door past the lady in the wheelchair and pedaled out of there like he was being chased by the police. He saw Silvia again a week later and offered her the same deal, but this time he brought a friend. Silvia went for it with no hesitation and this became a weekly ritual for about seven months.

Here it was years later, and Silvia was sitting right next to him in the car buying crack from him. She looked horrible and looking at her now made him cringe inside thinking that he used to have sex with her. She had dried up sores on her face, she looked like she had lost fifty pounds and not in a good way. Her hair was greasy as if she hadn't washed it in weeks and her fingernails had some black substance underneath. Silvia knew better than to ask if he wanted to have sex with her now, she knew how bad she looked, she simply stopped caring. The pull of drugs was greater than her own self- worth.

CHAPTER FOURTEEN

"What up Silvia? You alright?" he asked as he drove off towards the nearest store. For her to just jump in his car then get back out would look suspicious. So, every time he brought her something he made it seem like she needed a ride to the store. She counted out $900 and he gave her two grams shy of a whole ounce. He knew she wouldn't actually weigh out what she's buying, so it wouldn't be a problem that he was shorting her. As soon as he drove up to the store and stopped, she got out.

"Thanks baby! I'll call you at the end of the week. This better be some good shit too, last week it wasn't so great." she said, closing the car door behind her.

"Okay, do that!" he said out the window as he drove off, calling his next customer, who was also his mom.

Carlos's mom had been smoking crack since he was a baby. She wasn't stopping for no one and she didn't care what anyone thought or had to say. Carlos knew how much she was spending on dope, so he started serving her.

This had been going on for a couple of years, although sometimes Carlos had to admit to himself, that he did feel bad about selling his own mom crack. He got to the point where he understood that if she didn't get it from her son, she'd get it from someone else's son. At least with him, he knew he was giving her good shit, and not coated with some chemical that would kill her.

When he arrived, she was sitting on the porch waiting. She came running to the car, yelling as usual. "Damn, where was you at? I been calling you all day! I'ma stop fucking with your ass! I called you three hours ago and you told me you was on your way!"

"Look, I had some important shit to do," he said tired of the same old song and dance with her.

"What? Getting your bootie call? You talk to yo' daddy?" she asked, getting in the car.

"Naw not lately, why?"

"I seen him the other day. He still trying to get back with me," she said smiling like she was still in high school or something.

"When I call him, he don't ever answer the phone, so I don't even bother to call him anymore. Who's in there with you?" Carlos asked, seeing a few people passing by in the window.

"Just some friends. We about to get our barbecue on today! You see this nice ass weather we got don't you?" she asked, with one foot in the car and the other on the pavement.

"Yeah, it's going to be a nice day for that."

Seeing the look on his face she asked, "You wanna come in and eat? There's plenty of food."

"Naw, I'm good. I got other people to see today," he said as he got her sack together. It was sad to see his own mom as a crack head, but Carlos had gotten over that stage years ago of worrying and feeling guilty. Although she only wanted an ounce, he gave her an ounce and a half for only $800. Basically, she got the half for free which made her super happy.

"How's my grandbaby?" she asked as an afterthought, getting out of the car.

"He's getting real big mama," Carlos said, starting the car up.

"Here ya' go son," she said, throwing money in his lap and grabbing the bag of crack. "See ya' later!" she said running inside as quickly as possible to chase that first hit.

Carlos just shook his head and drove off. On the way back home he counted the money she gave him while stopped at a red light. She was short $120. *Same old shit*, he thought to himself.

On his way home, his phone rang. It was Olivia. "What's up mami?"

"Nothing what you doing? You got anything up for today?" she asked, sounding sexy.

"Shit, nothing really, just chilling! Why, what's good?"

"What you trying to do?"

"Nothing too much, I was gonna bring over my twin sister tonight for your boy Omies. I think he'll like her," Olivia said.

"Okay, that's cool. But let me call him first and make sure he don't have any other plans going on tonight."

"Yeah, you do that. Make sure he don't have any of them crazy girls popping up tonight, because they'll get their ass maced."

Carlos laughed at her toughness. "You ain't gotta worry about that, that fool set them straight. Ain't no drama happening, but let me call him and I'll call you back later and let you know what up, cool?"

"Why you gotta go? You got someone else over there?" she asked jokingly, not really caring if he did or not. He was very respectful towards her and treated her very well, so she wasn't trying to mess that up. For all she knew, she had herself a good looking and hardworking man, a hard thing to find. She had no idea he was selling drugs. He spent money on her, but not enough to cause her to look at him like he was a drug dealer. She figured he was just a hard-working Puerto Rican lover boy who had looks to kill. Omies on the other hand, looked very much like a drug dealer. He was always wearing very expensive clothes and shoes. He drove a nice, expensive car, big diamonds in each ear that you could see shining a mile away. And the chain he wore was just as ridiculous. It was at least eight carats of ice. Even though that wasn't her taste, she definitely knew her sister would be into him.

By the time Carlos got off the phone with Olivia he had just arrived home. Walking in the front door he saw Omies passed out, sleeping on the couch.

"Wake yo' sorry ass up nigga!" he said, slapping Omies leg.

"What's up?" Omies asked, opening his eyes a little bit. "You done cooking all that shit up?" Carlos asked, sitting in the recliner.

"That's what you woke me up for? Hell yeah! I been done. Man, that shit some A-1" Omies said, getting off the couch and walking to the fridge.

"Yeah, I know it's some good shit. And no that ain't why I woke you up. I got someone that wants to meet you."

"Hell naw, I ain't doing another blind date nigga. The last time you said that you brought some heifer from the suburbs to meet me. That bitch was almost three hundred pounds," Omies, said shaking his head no, remembering how heavy that girl was.

CHAPTER FIFTEEN

"Dogg, its Olivia's sister. Her twin sister," Carlos said, drawing him a mental picture of what Olivia looked like.

"What she look like? How old is she? Just cause she's her twin don't mean she's fine muthafucka! You seen her?" Omies asked, still suspicious that he was being set up on a dummy mission.

"She's 23 and single, with no kids dogg! I ain't seen her but Olivia said you'd like her," Carlos said, knowing Omies liked Olivia. "Why you care how old she is? You going to wife her up? Olivia said they was identical, so you know she's fine. You want me to make this happen or not?" Carlos asked tired of the twenty-one questions.

"I'm just asking, I see you all in love with Olivia's lil' ass, she been over here the last few nights," Omies said joking with him.

"Man, that's my baby! I might get that bitch pregnant. We gonna have some fine ass kids."

"What? Nigga you stupid! You already got one son with a crazy ass baby mama that you can't even control. You better put her in check first before you even think about knocking up Olivia or anyone else for that matter, before she fuck around and kill you both." Omies said. They looked at each other, and bust out laughing at the thought.

"Man, she been straight lately" Carlos said, defending her.

"Yeah, cause you been fucking her and bring her money and shit every day. I wouldn't be tripping either if I was her, but you bring in another baby mama, that is a whole other level of tripping. Right now you paying all the bills and she ain't working plus you paying her car note."

"Man, I'm doing all that shit for my son," Carlos said, explaining himself.

"Dog, I ain't even about to jump down your throat on that again, but you betta' wake up and smell the coffee. That bitch shitting all over you dog. You can't even see your son when you want to. She don't let you get him for the weekend or nothing!"

Carlos just ignored him as always and changed the subject. "Man, do you wanna meet Olivia's sister tonight or what? I ain't got all day!"

"Yeah, call them and have them meet us at the Hilton Suite tonight at 7:00p.m." Omies told him, already thinking of what he was gonna wear to impress her.

Omies jumped out of the shower and got dressed. He slipped on his all black expensive pants, a matching red, black, and white shirt, with his all black Gucci loafers. He put on his iced-out, white gold chain, his equally iced-out watch, his white-gold 4 carat pinkie ring, 2 ½ carat white-gold earrings, and his $4000 Cartier glasses to top it off. After he was done splashing on his cologne, he grabbed his pistol from under his pillow and an ounce of crack out of his drawer, and went over to Sasha's new apartment that he had just gotten for her.

Everything in it was new, from the 65" 4k Samsung TV that was on the wall, the marble end tables, leather couches, to the kitchen and bathroom fixtures. Omies had hooked her up and Sasha was feeling good. She only made $1,300 a month, but she was fine because she had Omies wrapped around her finger. He stayed spending money on her nonstop. And all Sasha was doing was putting her checks in the bank. She didn't need to spend her money on nothing because Omies paid for everything she had or wanted.

"Boy, you coulda' knocked!" Shareal, said walking out of the bathroom with a pink towel wrapped around her, while she dripped water and soap suds from the shower onto the off-white carpet.

"Knock? I got a key!" Omies said, checking her out. Shareal was Sasha's little sister, 18 years old 5'5", tight body with a nice booty and a gorgeous face. She could be a model. "What time Sasha get off work today?" he asked her, not taking his eyes off her for a second.

"I think she get off later tonight, probably midnight," she replied. "What you come here for if you knew she wasn't here?" Shareal asked him with a little attitude.

"Stay outta grown folks business. I came through to get the charger for my phone," he said. "Why you even questioning a nigga? You act like you live here or something! Who was that one girl you was with that day I seen you at the mall making light conversation."

"That's my friend Elesha, why?" she asked, crossing her arms over her chest.

"Shit, I just asked. What she say about a nigga? I seen her looking and shit, like she wanted to give a nigga some pussy," Omies said with a smile on his face.

"She ain't say nothing! I told her you was my sister's boyfriend and she left it like that... Niggas ain't shit! Look at you trying to get with my friend," Shareal said, laughing at him, shaking her head.

Omies laughed too, "It is what it is! As long as she ain't running her mouth, it's only some pussy! Your sister know I love her ass to death. She know a nigga' be fucking tho!"

"Oh, is that so? So If I ask her that's what she gonna say?" Shareal asked, rolling her eyes at him and his story.

"Yeah...Hell yeah, she know I be fucking!"

"Well that ain't what I heard. When she be telling me about you, she said you ain't been with no one but her, besides that bitch Hillary, who scratched her face up!" Shareal said, reminding him of the last fight.

CHAPTER SIXTEEN

"Well shit, that's even better, if she think that! Come here," Omies said, pulling her by the arm, but she quickly snatched back from him.

"Boy, you better gone somewhere."

"Oh, I can't see your little body? You know you want to show me how fine you is," Omies said walking close up on her.

"Boy what? You straight savage! I'm tellin' my sister," she said, going into the room and closing the door.

"Shareal, chill out!" Omies said, following her into the room, getting a little nervous about her saying anything to Sasha. "Damn, you gonna tell on me?"

"Yup! You shouldn't be so disrespectful! Yup, sho' is tellin'." She spat out at him.

"Aw for real? You gone play me like that?" he asked, wondering how he was gonna keep her ass quiet.

"Yup! You played me like I was some kind of hoe!" she said, sitting on the bed with her legs crossed, still wearing only a towel.

You are a hoe, stupid bitch, he thought. "I was just playing with you! My bad if I offended you. I apologize for that shit! You accept my apology?" he asked, standing in front of her.

She could smell his cologne and the baby lotion he mixed with it. His chain was shining from the sunlight coming through the window and the bling from his ring was nearly blinding her.

"Yeah, I guess I accept it, if you really mean it," she said with an attitude, not even sure he did mean it.

"So you ain't gonna tell your sister on me?" he asked, pulling out a big wad of money, probably the biggest wad she had ever seen. He had hundreds, fifties, twenties and tens rolled up. Her eyes grew as big and her face started to turn red.

"N..N..No, I'm not!" she said, stuttering so badly because her eyes were transfixed on the money he was counting out.

"Why you stuttering? What you scared of, money or something?"

She smacked her lips and rolled her eyes, "Boy please, I ain't scared of nothing!" she said with an attitude.

"What that mean?"

"I ain't scared of nothing, simply what I said, and why you so damn close to me? Back up! You trying to get me to rob you?" she joked nervously at how close he was to her.

"Damn, you gonna rob a nigga'?" he asked her holding his hands up.

"I might you keep showing off your money!" she threatened, cocking her index finger and thumb like a gun.

"How you gonna do that? You better have a real gun or something, or I'm folding your little ass up!" he joked back, and they both laugh.

"How much I gotta give you?" he asked, pressing forward.

CHAPTER SEVENTEEN

"Boy, what?"

"Calm your fine ass down! You heard what I said. I know you need money for something. How much you need?" he asked, unfolding some bills.

"I already told you I wasn't telling on you. Besides, you don't have what I need. I just got my license and I need money for a car!"

"How much is that?" he said unfolding more bills from his wad.

"$2,000 is the down payment! What, you gonna give it to me?" she asked, rolling her pretty little eyes again thinking he was full of it.

"It depends."

"On what?" she smacked her lips and ran her tongue over them.

"I mean $2,000 is a nice amount of money. How bout since you playing hard ball and shit, because I fuck with your sister, I'll give you $500 right now if you let me put my dick in you for 5 seconds."

She thought about going off on him again, but then that $500 sounded really good to her. $500 would go a long way to getting her a car, and he was only asking for 5 seconds.

"Nigga' you is crazy! Are you serious?" she asked, trying to find out if he was serious before she said anything.

Omies was wondering what was going on inside her head. He began peeling off bills on the bed. "That's $500 right there," he said, watching her glance down at all five of the hundred-dollar bills spread out on the lavender bed spread.

Omies saw her wavering and decided to peel off another bill, making it $600.

Oh my God! This nigga' is really serious, what the fuck! I can't. I can't do this! No, fuck him! He dirty, I'm tellin' Sasha, she thought.

Omies peeled 4 more bills making it an even $1000. Shareal was just sitting there in deep thought, and he knew how unsure she was because of how long she was taking to answer.

"Take this stack or fuck it! I'm tired of begging. I'm trying to put some money in your pockets! Talking bout you need money for a car, you aint trying to get a car. Where the fuck you gone get a thousand dollars cash in less than a minute?" he snarled at her, his dick was hard and ready.

"Okay, five seconds nigga', that's it!" She said, revealing her body to him by removing the towel slowly. Her pussy was cleanly shaved. She sat back on her bed ready.

"10 seconds now, I added another $500, remember? That's a whole thousand!" Omies said to her unbuckling his belt.

"Whatever, you full of shit nigga'!" she said as Omies dropped his pants and his dick sprung out and stood straight up. Shareal hadn't ever seen a dick that big before.

"Yeah nigga, you got 10 seconds and that's it!" she said as Omies crawled on the bed, in between her legs and pulled them wider.

"Put it in there for me," he told her. Shareal grabbed his dick and rubbed it against her pussy lips, making herself wet, then she stuck it inside. She was tight. Omies moved very slow and easy as he entered her but made sure he stuck every inch deep down inside her.

"Wheww!" she moaned out, "It's too big!" she said jumping back and away from his dick, making him fall out of her.

"Come on, stop playing! We was almost done," he said reaching for her legs and pulling her back to him.

"Uh, uh! It's too big! I can't take all of that!" she said covering her pussy up with the towel.

"Okay, I ain't gonna put it all the way in this time. I thought you was straight. See, now I know how deep I can go, come here," he said pulling the towel away and spreading her legs apart again. He put his dick back inside her. She started counting. "One, twooo, threeee... Ah... three.. f..our..fiveee. Ah, ah, ah," she started moaning louder and louder as he started stroking her faster. "Okay, okay! Stop! Don't stop, please don't stop! I'm bout to ...!" she moaned in between each stroke. She soon went silent and tensed up as she released her fluids all over his dick. Her body went limp and she pushed him off of her, without letting him even get a nut. *Oh my God,* she thought to herself. Her legs were shaking still. *Oh my God!* was all she could say to herself.

Omies had gotten up and was already in the bathroom jacking off, finishing what he started. Even though he didn't nut while fucking, he was still satisfied. He knew she'd come crawling back for more.

Later that day Omies picked up Carlos and they were on their way to the Hilton Hotel with a half-gallon of Patron. They had Olivia and her twin sister meet them there. When they arrived, they saw both of them waiting in a parking spot. Omies drove up next to them and they got out looking like celebrities. Omies could see both of their faces light up with surprise. They both got out and Olivia introduced her sister to Omies. She could see her sister was digging him right away, and Omies was definitely digging her right back. Olivia and her sister really were identical.

Damn, I wonder if they ever fucked the same dudes before. They look too much alike. Shit, if I was a twin, my brother would be in trouble, Omies thought to himself, wondering what it was like to have a threesome with both of them. They all walked up to the room, which was a two bedroom suite, with two Jacuzzis and one, big living room and kitchen area. They walked into the living room which featured some surrealist painting that covered the entire back wall. The girls were excited about the spacious suite. The glass windows all around the room were immaculately polished as they were looking down at the city from the 20th floor.

"So why don't you have a man? You way too fine to be single, what's the catch?" Omies asked while pouring up a shot of Patron.

"There is no catch honey, I'm single because I haven't found the right man, not boy, to settle down with," she replied sipping her drink slowly.

"Well, what kind of man you looking for? Maybe I know someone?" "Just somebody who respects me, cares for me and who's doing something positive with themselves and somebody who has time for me in his life. You know someone like that?" she asked, moving her hand away from his.

"That's it? You ain't looking for a nigga to take care of you?" Omies asked.

Is that a trick question? Resa thought to herself. *Of course, but you won't find that out any time soon Slick Rick!* "No honey, I have my own! I work hard every day for mine," she told him arrogantly. "I don't need your money baby!"

Resa was digging Omies swag, his wardrobe, the jewelry he had on, but she could tell this was going to be the same shit she went through with Dayshawn. She knew Omies was a drug dealer and she knew he had lots of females chasing him around.

"So what do you do?" Resa asked, as if she didn't already know.

"I work at a dealership part time and I throw parties at clubs sometimes too," Omies said, lying through his teeth.

"Oh, okay! That's pretty cool!" Resa said, letting him think she believed him.

"What do you do."

"I work at a nursing home and a hospital. I take care of elderly people. Its straight and it pays the bills. I'm also going to school to become a nurse," she said proudly, knowing he had her pegged for some gas station clerk or something. She saw the surprise in his eyes.

All these hoes trying to be nurses, he thought. "Okay, that's what's up baby girl! You got a little something going on in your life. I like that...what about kids? Do you have any?" Omies asked, knowing she had to have some kids.

CHAPTER EIGHTEEN

Surprising him again she said, "Nope, no kids. At least not yet. Do you have any?"

"Yeah, I have 6 kids. 3 boys and 3 girls," Omies said watching her reaction. Resa was real quiet trying to process how many were from different mothers.

"How many baby mamas, and how old are you?" she asked, turned off completely now.

"4 baby mamas and I'm 24! What's wrong with that?" Omies asked.

Resa poured a stiff shot of Patron and took a big swallow. "Oh, nothing, never mind!" she said grabbing a remote and channel surfing. *This conversation is over, she thought.*

"Resa!" Omies called her name softly.

"What?" she asked, turning around with a attitude.

"I'm just playing with you! I don't have any kids," he told her smiling.

Resa laughed a little and said, "Say you swear Omies!"

"I swear I was just seeing how you was gonna react. Ask Carlos if you don't believe me," he said, still smiling at her.

"Well you seen I was pissed and turned off! I don't play that baby mama drama shit."

"Damn for real? You was gonna X a nigga out because of some kids?"

"Um, yeah! I don't want no nigga' with 6 kids and 5 baby mamas or however many you said you had. Fuck that! I wanna nigga' with no kids, so we can build our own family together."

"Right, right, I feel you. So basically what you saying is, you gonna let me take care of you and be your baby daddy?"

"I've already told you, I can take care of myself!"

"Okay then, except for taking care of you?"

"You wanna be my baby daddy?" *this boy is tripping*, she thought to herself, *he don't even know me.* "You don't even know me and you already talking about kids? Nigga please! Lord, you must be crazy!"

Omies started laughing at her dramatics, "Naw, naw, it ain't like that. I'm just feeling you, and I can see myself settling down with somebody like you. Real talk!"

"Aww, is that how you get females out of their panties, by selling them dreams?" Resa joked.

"Damn! For real? See, now you clowning me! Okay, okay be like that!" Omies said, scooting away from Resa a little, like he was done with her.

Resa started laughing at his antics and asked, "I know you didn't just move away from me? Come here, come back, I was just messing with you." She moved by him, grabbing his head and laying it on her chest. "Aww boo, I'm sorry. I didn't know you was so sensitive," she said, kissing him on his forehead. "Is that better you little baby?"

Omies laughed and snuggled up against her. "Yeah, that's better, don't be doing me like that. I have no reason to lie. If I ain't feeling you, I'ma let you know."

"Whatever, you nigga's run that same game, but I bet if I dropped these panties right now, your dick would be right out, ready to fuck!"

"I get plenty of that. If it happens, it happens. Right now I'm more interested in getting to know who you are, cause

I'm digging you! You fine as hell, you doing something with your life. You independent and it seems like you got a good head on your shoulders."

"Okay, okay, that sounds good, I feel the same way. I'm digging you also."

Olivia and Carlos was already in their room, soaking in the Jacuzzi with their clothes off. "I miss you boo," Olivia said, kissing him on the lips.

"I missed you too," Carlos replied, loving the Jacuzzi. The water was hot and bubbly. "You think your sister will like Omies?"

"Yeah, I know she will. He is exactly her type," she said, kissing him on his neck.

"That's what's up then. You betta' not tell her about what happened that day when his hoes was tripping on him."

"Too late!" she said with a smile.

"Aww, you out cold! You hated on the nigga' already?"

"No, no I didn't! He straight, watch! I know she going to like him," Olivia told him, then she started swirling her tongue inside his mouth, making him forget all about Omies and his issues.

The next morning the four of them left the room before noon.

"Nice to meet you Resa, I'll call you later on tonight," Omies told her in the parking lot.

"Nice to have met you too. I had fun!" Resa said, hugging him before she drove away with Olivia.

On the way home Omies commented, "Good looking on that shit. Ol' girl banging dogg," he said to Carlos giving him a pound.

"I told you, I got you dog!" Carlos said, smiling and laying back as he fired up a blunt of kush.

"Man, they look just alike, same every fucking thing! Booty, titties and all." They both laughed.

"Man, I ain't never seen nothing like it since the double mint twins." Carlos said passing the blunt.

"I got up early this morning to piss right?"

"Yeah, so?"

"My shit was burning like a muthafucka'! And when I got through, my shit was leaking some yellow shit," Omies said, looking at Carlos's reaction which was a laugh.

"Nigga' you got that sauce!" he said still laughing and coughing up smoke at the same time.

"Sauce? What sauce? I ain't got no damn sauce." Omies said looking all confused.

"Nigga', that sauce!" Carlos said, still laughing and making no sense to Omies.

"What the fuck is sauce?" Omies asked, getting irritated now.

"Nigga you got Gonorrhea! That shit ain't no joke either! I had that shit a couple times and it hurts. You betta' hit up the clinic ASAP!" Carlos advised him, looking serious.

"I'ma fuck one of these hoes up!" Omies said, pissed.

"Don't get mad at the female, wear a condom! You can get that just by fucking multiple females raw. If you mix different body fluids together, sometimes you can create an STD or bacterial infection. Just think about it, all them different pussy juices getting inside one small pee hole," Carlos said, breaking it down.

"Who the fuck is you, Dr. OZ muthafucka'? Man this some crucial shit, my shit leaking like a muthafucka'!" Omies complained rubbing his dick through his pants.

"You fuck Resa last night?"

"Naw nigga'! She wasn't trying to give it up. Bitch was playing. It's going to take some time, but I'ma get it. Well, at least that's the way it seems. I tried though, she wasn't having it."

"Well her sister was the opposite. I got her ass off the Patron and it was a wrap," Carlos bragged, laughing along with Omies.

"Man, fuck all that! I need to find out who gave me this shit," Omies said thinking back to who he hit.

"Shit. The last bitch you fucked. Gonorrhea don't take long to show up, day or two sometimes. You could be pissing razors the next morning. So, who you fuck yesterday?" Carlos asked, thinking he was going to say Sasha.

"Dog, you ain't gonna believe me when I tell you! Guess?"

"I don't know... Sasha?" Carlos said, guessing the obvious choice.

"Her little sister Shareal."

"Shut the fuck up! That little bitch burnt you?" Carlos asked, shocked beyond belief.

"I guess. She was the last one I fucked, and it was only for a few seconds."

"I knew that little bitch was wild! Do she got some good pussy, I wanna hit that hoe next."

They both laughed.

"Hell yeah she do, but that hoe nasty dog! I ain't got that bitch number to get in touch with her either." "Ask Sasha, just tell her I want the number!" Carlos said, thinking of a way to get her number.

"I will just not today, she already gonna be mad, because I ain't answer my phone all night."

"Just take yo' ass to the clinic and catch Shareal when you can."

"o what you think of Carlos's friend Omies?" Olivia asked Resa as they drove from the hotel.

"Girl, he cute as hell! I like his little corn ball personality too." Resa said, thinking about last night.

"Yep, I know, but be careful though. Obviously you know he's a dope boy and I don't want you getting hurt."

"Yeah, I know. But you know there ain't a lot of niggas around that ain't in the dope game. So I really can't run too far from it."

"Yeah, I guess you right." Olivia replied, "Just be careful though."

"I will, you ain't got to worry about me...so where the hell you been? Kareem said he hasn't talked to you or seen you in about 4 or 5 months," Resa said.

"Girl, the last time I talked to Kareem, he wanted me to set some fool up from Chicago. Him asking me to do that scandalous shit told me that he don't give a fuck about no one but himself. Don't get me wrong, I love Kareem, we family and all, but big brother or not, why would you put me in the middle of some shit like that? You know?"

"Maybe he had a good ass plan where nothing bad was going to happen to you or something? You know Kareem's word is his bond!" Resa said.

"Forget that! I aint setting no one up! People get killed doing stuff like that. He needs to sit his lazy ass down and find a real job. Yeah, he got my back until I go to jail or get shot messing around with his dumb ass!" Olivia said, fed up with Kareem, always looking for the easy way out.

"I agree, but you know Kareem's hard-headed ass ain't about to work a 9-5 job," Resa said.

Olivia finally arrived at a gas station to drop Resa off. Whoever she was meeting was driving a ruby red Cadillac truck on big rims. The rims were chrome and ruby red to match the truck.

"Dang girl, who is that?" Olivia asked.

"His name Dayshawn. He cool and shit, but we just friends. I'll call you in a couple of days and we'll get together and go see Carlos and Omies, okay?" Resa asked, grabbing her purse on the way out.

"Okay, call me! Love you, be careful," Olivia yelled out.

"Okay, love you too!"

Omies and Carlos went to the clinic and were sitting there for about 2 hours. The nurse called them both to the back to give them their results. Carlos was negative which he figured. Omies was positive for Chlamydia and Gonorrhea. The nurse gave him a powder drink mixed with water, 1 pill and a prescription he would have to take for seven days, 2 pills a day.

On the way home, Omies stopped at a car wash to get a quick wash. A ruby red Cadillac truck was stopped in front of them, with a license plate that spelled, "Dayshawn."

"Look at Dayshawn, that nigga stay washing his cars!" Omies said, paying the attendant for the works.

"He must of just got that truck, ain't that the same plate he had on the Navigator he was driving?" Carlos asked, rolling a blunt up.

"Yup, that nigga' be doing his thang, he keep a female with him. I bet he got one in there right now giving him some head," Omies said, "I should get out and holla at him real fast."

Up ahead in the truck, Resa saw Omies BMW in the side view mirror. *Aw shit! I hope he don't know Dayshawn!* Resa thought to herself. *Good thing Dayshawn's windows have tint on them.* The car in front of them pulled out the port and Dayshawn pulled in, buying her a little time.

"What you been doing all night, looking all rough and shit?" Dayshawn asked, staring at her and her wrinkled clothes that looked like they had been slept in.

"Nothing, just chilling with my sister and them."

"Them? Them who? Some dudes?"

"Yeah, some of her friends. I didn't know them niggas though, I was just there drinking."

"I just seen Olivia out last week with a nigga named Carlos. I thought they was husband and wife by the way they was holding hands through the mall. You know who I'm talking about? Carlos?" Dayshawn asked.

"Yeah, yeah that's who it was. You know them or something?" She asked, worried a little. She didn't need niggas swapping stories about her.

"Yeah, Carlos and Omies. Yeah I know them niggas. You be fucking with Omies?" Dayshawn asked surprised at how much she got around.

"Naw, I just met the nigga last night!"

"Oh, I was about to say!"

"What?"

"Shit, that nigga' a nasty nigga and the Feds watching the nigga. Let me know if you gone be fucking with that nigga' or not, because I ain't trying to attract no Fed attention. That nigga be splurging and stunting so hard. That nigga hot as hell!" Dayshawn said.

Resa sat back and started thinking to herself. *I only knew Omies for one day and people telling me stuff about him already. He cool, cute, sexy and all, but I'm not trying to get caught up in no fed shit. I guess I might have to let this guy keep it moving. If he call, I'm not even answering it, or maybe I'll just get his money. Naw, forget that I might wind up liking him for real, then came the feds. Yeah, I'm definitely done with him.*

CHAPTER TWENTY

Dayshawn drove out of the car wash and put the car in park. He got out and started drying the truck off and spraying Armor All on the tires. Resa was sitting there hoping that Omies drove out of the wash before her and Dayshawn left. She even got out of the truck and walked around it, telling Dayshawn he missed a spot. She tried stalling him as much as possible, but Dayshawn was done pretty quick and was ready to go before Omies came out. Her plan didn't work. She figured if Omies saw her with Dayshawn he would never call her. She didn't want any more of her pictures in some DEA briefing room, talking about she was involved with Omies.

When Omies was done getting his wash he dried and then sprayed his tires with Armor All, just as Dayshawn had done. He knew Sasha was at work, but he was hoping that her sister Shareal was still over there. So he called the house phone.

"Hello, who this?" Omies asked when the phone was answered by a female.

"Who dis? You called here! Who is this?" The voice asked with attitude.

"This O', what up Shareal? Where your sister at?"

"She at work I think, call her cell phone."

"You there by yourself?" Omies asked, hoping she was.

"Yeah, you got some more money?"

"I wish you would! I ain't paying for that infected shit! Whoever you fucking, you betta start using a rubber, because that nigga' have Gonorrhea and Chlamydia!"

"Fuck you! I ain't got shit nigga'!" she yelled.

"Yeah, you do, I just left the clinic like 10 minutes ago. I'm just telling you to go get checked and cured. If you want me to, I'll take you to the clinic myself, right now! You wanna go?" Omies asked, calming her down.

"Yeah, come get me." she said, sounding upset.

"I'll be there in like 5 minutes, meet me downstairs."

I'ma drop my nigga off at the crib, then I'll be over there to come get you," Omies said, reassuring her that he was coming soon.

"Okay."

---

2 Weeks Later

Carlos had just got off work with his uncle, working construction. He drove to his baby mama's house because she told him earlier on the phone that he could come see his son. She also had asked him for $400 to pay her car note, but he told her he didn't have it. He was starting to take some of Omies advice into consideration.

He arrived at her aunt's house, who she stayed with.

Selena's car was sitting in the driveway, and her aunt's car was gone. First he knocked but got no answer.

Maybe they taking a nap, he thought as he started calling her cell phone and her aunt's phone too but still he didn't get no answer. *This bitch! I told her I was on my way! I coulda stayed at work and made some more money. I know her ass is in there.* Carlos kept knocking and calling, but still no one answered, so he began walking back to his car.

Selena was peeking out the window, holding the baby. *He can't give me no money, he can't see his son,* she said to herself.

Carlos hadn't seen his son in over a week, because Selena kept playing games with him. He dialed Omies phone.

"What up?"

"What's up man?" Carlos asked sounding upset.

"Shit, what's good? You alright?"

"Man this bitch keep playing games with me. I don't even know what to do. She gonna make me do something stupid to her ass!" Carlos threatened in frustration.

"Let me guess, you told her you wasn't giving her no money and now you can't see your son?"

"Yup! I shoulda' listened to you a long time ago!"

"I hate to say it, but I told you so. You fucked up bad having a baby with a bitch like that. Nigga' I ain't got no kids, so I can't tell you much. Call your dad and see what kind of advice he can give you, because that's fucked up. Maybe go to court and get some visitation that way," Omies suggested when he heard tears in Carlos's voice.

He loved his son and it tore him apart to not see him more.

"Alright I'ma holla' at you when I get there," Carlos said to Omies, embarrassed by the tears as he hung up. He dialed Selena's number again and screamed into the car and banged on the steering wheel with his fist. *I can't believe she doing me like this. She been doing it the whole time, no matter how cool I try to be. Bitch making me pay to see my own son.*

Carlos was pouring buckets of tears. He was in pain. It wouldn't stop hurting. Feeling like someone was constantly stabbing him in his stomach. He was beyond hurt at her betrayal. *How can a person you have a baby with treat you so bad? I never treated her bad. We only separated because I caught her cheating on me. All I did was be a good man to her and my baby.* His mind was racing a hundred miles an hour and his tears were falling even faster. He was gripping the steering wheel so hard his knuckles had turned purple.

Olivia was calling his phone and even though he needed someone to talk to, now was not the time to hear her bad mouthing Selena, it wouldn't help anything. He finally understood. Selena would let him see his son only if he was bringing her money.

Omies phone rang and he saw it was Sasha calling him again.

"Hello!"

"What's your problem?"

"What you mean, what's my problem?" he asked, hoping this wasn't going to turn into a fight. It had already been a messed up week.

"It's been a whole two weeks and you ain't been over here to even fuck me! That's unlike you, so tell me what the problem is? You gotta another girl, at least be man enough to tell me!"

"I've been busy that's all! A lot of shit been going on with me. It ain't no other girl so you can stop tripping about that shit!"

CHAPTER TWENTY-ONE

"**W**ell I need some dick! When you coming over here?"

Omies laughed at her, "I got you, I'll be over later, you freak!"

"Okay, oh I almost forgot to tell you the police found that security guard from my school body floating in the river. I guess someone killed him. They say he was shot 5 times."

"Damn, for real? That's fucked up."

"Yeah."

"Well, I'll be over there later. Be ready, daddy been missing his pussy!"

She laughed at the way his voice changed, "You better be ready, mama been feigning for her dick!"

"Shareal, you ready to go home?" she asked, yelling into the living room. Shareal had been over there since she moved in helping her unpack, but that had been done for over a week.

"Nooo, not today, please," she begged. She hate being at home because everyone was always trying to tell her what to do.

"Girl, I'm trying to get some dick tonight and I ain't having you stopping that. I need me some!" Sasha said completely unashamed.

"Go ahead! I ain't trying to stop you. I know you don't need this whole big ass apartment though," Shareal said, looking at her with puppy dog eyes, begging her to let her stay.

They both started laughing. "You just don't know. I might need every square inch."

"Oh my God! You look so stanky walking like that!" Shareal joked as she watched her sister switch away. "Can I stay sis? I'll stay out of the way, I promise," she said, pleading some more. "And who coming?"

"You know don't nobody get this besides O... You can stay I guess, but if he want you to leave, you gonna have to leave." she warned her little sister.

"Oh, well I'm good then. O' is my dog, he ain't gonna put me out," Shareal said, sounding really sure of herself.

"Oh, okay! We'll see about that." Sasha replied as she went into the bedroom to pick out something sexy to wear for him before she took a shower.

Shareal waited until she heard the water turn on and then she grabbed her phone, she had saved Omies number from her sister's caller ID.

"Hello?" Omies answered, he didn't recognize the number.

"Hey O', What you doing!?"

"Nothing, chilling! Who dis'?" he asked, recognizing the voice a little.

"This Shareal, I know you ain't forgot about me nigga."

"Oh, what up doe? Where you at?"

"At my sister's place, but she in the shower."

"What's good?"

"Nothing really, just wondering when me and you going to have some more time together? No charge this time. I want to make it up to you for giving you the STD," Shareal told him, feeling embarrassed still.

He laughed a little.

"This is not funny, I swear I didn't know."

"I feel you, I didn't think you did it on purpose and I ain't tripping, the shit gone now, you should be good too. I could come get you right now if you want me to. Walk down the street to that liquor store right on the corner. By the time you get there, I'll be pulling up."

"Mine is clear now too! I'm leaving right now," she said hanging up and grabbing her purse she had just bought. "I'ma go to the store, I'll be back later sis!" she yelled before she went out the door.

A few minutes later she was in his car. "What's up with you?" Omies asked her when she got in.

"You! Missing you!"

"Missing me? Yeah right! You ain't even let a nigga' fuck you long enough to miss me. I ain't bust or nothing. You cold! You robbed a nigga'," Omies said, squeezing her thigh.

"Well, you will bust this time!" Shareal said, smiling at him as she looked at his groin area.

As soon as they walked into Omies place they saw Carlos sitting on the couch talking on the phone. He sounded like he was in an important conversation.

Something about custody of his son. Shareal just waved at him and kept walking until Omies pointed out his room.

Omies slapped her on the booty as soon as she walked in and then he closed the door. Shareal was wearing a blue jean mini-skirt with some heels and no panties on. Omies's dick was hard the second the door shut. She didn't have to do anything but walk, he was ready. He walked behind her and bent her over the bed and inserted his dick into her already moist pussy, wasting no time.

"Ah shit!" she moaned when she felt his dick rubbing against her walls. He rolled her skirt up to her back and gripped her waist with his hands, then started stroking her. Her pussy became wetter and wetter and soon he felt himself about to cum. "Where you want this nut at?" he whispered.

"In me!" she moaned, but it was too late, Omies had already pulled out and nutted all over her caramel brown, ass cheeks. They both were out of breath. "Get me a towel," she said, as his juices made its way down her legs. "I don't know why you didn't just cum inside me?" she asked, wiping her ass and legs off.

"Cum inside you? You on birth control or something?"

"Yeah dummy!" she lied.

He wasn't buying it. He had heard that line by too many girls wanting to be taken care of. He didn't take chances like that.

"You ready?" he asked, pulling his pants back up.

"Ready for what?"

"For me to drop you back off!"

"Damn already? I can't have no more dick? I'll suck it for you," she said, looking desperate.

"I got something to do. I'll fuck with you tomorrow or something." he asked not really having anything to do, he just was ready to drop her back off because he got his nut and plus she was trouble. What if Sasha popped up or something?

"You bogus! I see how you playing it!" she said with a attitude.

"Damn that wasn't enough?"

"It's been two weeks and that was only like a minute!" she said, not at all satisfied.

"Go fuck Carlos, he in there!"

"What the fuck I look like? Fuck you O'! You ain't shit!" She said, starting to fix her skirt and hair. "Fuck you nigga'!"

Omies started laughing at her tantrum. "Chill out!" he said walking behind her as his pants dropped and his dick was in his hand rubbing it between her ass cheeks.

CHAPTER TWENTY-TWO

"**M**ove," she said, smiling and trying to get away from him until she felt his lips on her neck.

She arched her back, holding onto the dresser while sticking her booty out. Omies squeezed his dick back into her pussy while she was standing up. His dick was still leaking sperm from the first nut which made her pussy even wetter.

"Ah! Ow! Ah! Ah, owww! Ouch! Ouch!" she screamed for about 10 minutes as he punished her. This time it was painful for her as she got every inch she wanted. It felt like he was ripping her insides out, but yet it felt good to her at the same time. And still she came long and hard, while standing up. Her knees had buckled and she could barely stand when Omies was done with her. Her pussy felt swollen and it caused her to walk funny.

"Now let's go!" Omies demanded.

"Okay daddy, damn I'm coming," she said taking her heels off because she was having a hard time walking in them. She walked all the way to the parking lot with no socks or shoes on.

"Why you walking like that?"

"Boy stop! You know you just fucked the shit out of me!" She had a wide grin on her face.

Kareem was on his way to meet a dude he knew by the name of Gage. He had called Gage up to buy 2 kilos of cocaine, but he only had $33,000. Gage said it was straight and that Kareem could pay him the rest whenever he made it.

He soon arrived at the park where he was supposed to meet Gage. It was sunny and the weather was nice and warm. Females were everywhere, walking around half naked like it was a hundred degrees out. Kareem spotted Gage's car out of the thousands parked, so he drove over to him. Gage was sitting on the driver's side of his all white Ferrari and when he seen Kareem, he opened the door and stepped holding a Gucci bag.

"What's up playboy?" Gage said, jumping in with Kareem.

"What's up? You the playboy! You out here shitting on niggas in that Ferrari, God damn!"

They both started laughing as Kareem drove off to go park somewhere in the park so he could look at the cocaine without anyone seeing their business.

"Man, you should already know that's A-1 blood!" Gage assured him as he looked around carefully. Kareem started counting out money and Gage counted right after him. In the midst of them counting, the passenger door opened up and a hand reached in and held a pistol to Gage's chin.

"Put your hands on the steering wheel, or I'ma blow his head off, then yours! You wanna do this the hard way or the easy way?" the robber asked Kareem, while digging the pistol deeper into Gage's neck. The robber's face was hidden behind a black ski mask, and all you could see was the gold grill he had in his mouth. "Run all that shit!" The not too smart robber said. A grill like that was easily recognizable and Gage would never forget it.

Gage was shaking like he was about to have a seizure. "Give him all that shit nephew! Everything, don't even trip," Gage said to Kareem, trying to caution him about making a wrong move. Kareem acted unsure of what to do, so he started stuffing money into the Gucci bag, along with the 2 kilos of cocaine. To Gage, it wasn't that big of a deal, he had money. But he could tell by the look on Kareem's face that he was sick at what was happening and quite possibly broke.

"Thank you!" the robber said sarcastically as he ran off with their shit.

"Man, what the fuck was that!?" Kareem asked, punching the driver's door in anger.

"Dog, that's what I'm trying to figure out! You recognize that nigga'?" Gage asked looking in the direction the robber ran off towards.

"I will if I ever see that grill again! What you got nigga's following and watching you? Nigga', that's all I had! I ain't got a dollar to my name!" Kareem shouted.

"Man, I don't know, shit happens! But shoot back around to the car. I got a lil' something for you to work with. I apologize for this shit dog, real talk." Gage said, trying to make him feel a little better.

Kareem didn't say anything. He was quiet until he got back to Gage's car. Gage jumped out and came back with a Louis Vuitton bag. This one was smaller. "This is all I can do for now. This is a quarter kilo of cocaine and about $2,000, work this and get back with me, I got you. I need to make the money back I lost too. This is a dirty game we in and I know you mad, but we ain't got no control over some shit." Gage said handing Kareem the bag.

"Man, that's some bullshit. But alright. I'll get back to you when I sell this shit." Kareem said as he drove off and headed home. It seemed like it took forever to get there because he had to do the speed limit with that much dope on him. When he got inside, he sat down and dialed Slim's number, but it went straight to voicemail. *Where that nigga' at?* he thought to himself. Then he heard a knock at the door, it was Slim!

"Damn nigga'! I beat you here, what the fuck was you doing?" Kareem asked with a big smile on his face. "I bet your scary ass did 20mph all the way here," he said jokingly as he rubbed his hands together in excitement.

CHAPTER TWENTY-THREE

"**H**ell yeah I did! I ain't trying to get swooped up with 2 kilos," Slim said, laying the Gucci bag full with money and dope on the table. "What that nigga' say when I was gone?" Slim asked wanting to hear all the details on how Gage bitched up.

"Shit! That nigga' was looking dumb as hell. I was tripping though. In the end he gave me a quarter bird for free and $2,000. Nigga' I laughed all the way home. But next time, don't wear your grill dumb ass nigga."

Slim took his grill out and threw it in the trash.

"Dog, I was talking to my sister today," Kareem said, pocketing his half of the cash.

"And? What she talking about?"

"Shit, nothing really! But she did tell me that Dayshawn got a new truck, a Cadillac Escalade on some 26's!"

"That nigga' must of traded that Navigator in!"

"Naw, that nigga' still got that Navigator, Resa driving that now."

"So that nigga' tried playing us?" Slim asked, referring to Dayshawn again.

"Man that nigga' did play us!"

"Aw, he got it coming again then! This time we gonna tie that muthafucka' up and make him cough up everything!" Slim said pissed that they didn't get everything he had. "In fact, we need to run up in Gage's shit too!"

"Right, right! But nobody know where that muthafucka' stay at!"

One Week Later

Omies and Carlos were at home relaxing, when Carlos asked if he had heard from Resa.

"Hell naw man! She don't even answer when I call her cell phone! Call Olivia and ask her what up," Omies said, nodding to his cell phone siting on the couch, next to the remote.

"Man, she probably ain't feeling you! Did you ever think of that?" Carlos asked.

"Nigga' please! That bitch was feeling me for sho'!" Omies said, not believing she wasn't into him.

"Well why she ain't call then?"

"Nigga you high? Why you fucking with me!"

"I ain't fucking with you. I'm being for real! I just thought your game was a little stronger playa! What happened to that long romantic night y'all shared, talking 'til three in the morning?"

Omies laughed, "Call Olivia and see what's up."

Seeing he wasn't going to let it die, Carlos picked up his phone and called Olivia's number. "Hello?"

"What's up baby?"

"Nothing about to go pick up Resa."

"Then what you gonna do?" Carlos asked, wondering how he was gonna approach the subject of Omies hurt ego.

"We about to go to the mall and eat."

"Can me and O' go with ya'll? Our treat!"

"It's up to Resa. I don't think she wants to get involved with Omies, because she heard that the Feds was watching him."

"What? The Feds? Who told her some shit like that?" Carlos asked, standing up now.

"I don't know! Some guy she be dealing with!"

Carlos was paranoid now and peered out the blinds looking for suspicious or unknown cars. "What's his name?"

"Carlos I don't know him!"

"Well do you know what he drive? How you gonna hear something like that and not ask questions knowing I fucks with O'?" Carlos asked her, not caring if she got mad.

"A red Lac truck and he has a Navigator too I think."

"Dayshawn? Is that his name?"

"Yup, I think that's who it is. You know him?"

"Aw hell naw! When you pick your sister up, come through." He was pissed.

"She going to be mad at me if I do that!" Olivia protested, not wanting to get in the middle.

"She'll be okay, bring her through." Carlos reassured her he needed to get to the bottom of this.

Olivia hung up the phone thinking she had just started some shit. Resa got in the car as she rolled to a stop. She was looking beautiful and ready for a trip to the mall to do some shopping courtesy of Dayshawn's wallet.

"Hey girl!" Resa greeted her sister.

"Hey!" was all Olivia could muster out.

"What's wrong with you?" she asked, knowing something was up.

"Nothing," Olivia lied, not knowing how to say it. She knew Resa would be mad because she went and repeated something, she told her. "Something wrong, so why lie? Tell me what it is." Resa pressed her sister, thinking it was something bad.

"I just got off the phone with Carlos and he wants me to stop by real quick. Omies been trying to call you."

"Aw hell naw! Turn around and drop me off, I ain't going!" Resa snapped on her sister.

"Please, just go! I told Carlos what you said about the Feds and he was tripping!"

"Why you even tell him that shit? You gonna pick some nigga over yo' sister?" Resa was pissed.

"I..I don't know! He was wondering why you didn't answer the phone for Omies when he call. I told him I didn't want to get in the middle of this bullshit. Then he asked what bullshit I was talking about," Olivia explained what she said to him.

"That's fucked up. Now they about to be on Dayshawn's head," Resa said, then she seen her phone ringing, it was Dayshawn. "I'm not answering, fuck that! See what you got started? You need to stop talking so damn much, that was between us!"

"You might as well answer, you gonna have to hear it anyways eventually. I didn't know it was a secret and why wouldn't I tell my man to be careful about something that might get him in trouble? They both live together so any dope they find there will fall on both of them." Olivia said but she saw Resa was just ignoring her. They rode in silence all the way to Omies and Carlos's place.

"This where Omies and Carlos live?" Resa asked her sister, breaking the silence.

"Yeah, why?"

"Wow, Kareem stay over here too."

"For real?" Olivia said, looking around the street for her brother's car.

They got out and walked up to the door and Olivia knocked. Omies opened the door and waved them inside. "How y'all doing?" he asked as they came in and stood around. Omies was sitting on the couch, just looking at them.

"Fine!" they both said in unison. Olivia got up and went to Carlos's room, while Resa sat on the couch.

"What's good Resa? You out cold, why you ain't tell me what was up? You just gonna let a nigga get popped by the Feds?" Omies asked her, not wasting anytime with small talk.

CHAPTER TWENTY-FOUR

R esa was quiet for a minute before she responded. "Because I didn't want to start no drama!"

"Well that's already started now. Are you trying to fuck with me or not? Ain't no fucking Feds watching me! I'm good, and you ain't gotta worry about nothing like that anyways. That nigga Dayshawn a hating ass nigga."

"Nigga' you are tripping thinking I'm not trying to fuck with you!" Resa said laughing at the look on his face. "For real, I wanna fuck with you, but..," she started to say when Omies interrupted her.

"But what? What you worried about?"

"Honestly? Me falling in love with your ass and then you going to jail or getting murdered in a drug deal gone bad." Resa said, slicing him right into the chest with those words.

"But that could happen to anybody out here. You can't hold your feelings in check because of that!"

"But you a high risk nigga'! Look at how you dress, what you drive! It screams to everybody come rob me, I got dope money for the taking! Nigga's know you got money and they going to try to rob you and maybe kill you for it!" Resa said, thinking of Kareem and Slim.

"So what? You want me to dress like a bum ass nigga'?"

"Naw, but just slow down. Look at Carlos, he don't dress like a bum or a dealer. It's scary the way you feel like you have to splurge. It's just too much! At least get a legitimate business with the money so you can get out eventually! What, you just going to continue to sell dope until you go to prison or get killed? Everyone gets caught eventually!"

"So if a nigga' got a legit business out here, I can have you?" Omies asked, moving closer to her on the couch.

"Have me? Yeah, if you tone your splurging down and get a real business, yes you can have me Omies," she said, smiling at him and accepting his kiss.

"Bet! I'm on that shit tomorrow!" Omies promised as Resa started laughing at him, then they hugged.

This nigga think it's a game, Resa thought to herself.

"Oh and stop fucking with that hoe-ass nigga' Dayshawn too!" Omies said.

"Why? We just friends," she said carefully, knowing he didn't like Dayshawn.

"Fuck that nigga'! You see him hating on me! Who knows how many other people he done told that to! That's some bitch ass shit there!" Omies said getting mad all over again.

Weighing her options in her head, Resa said, "We'll see. I might though."

"What you mean you might? Okay then,"

"What? We cool, that's all it is!"

"Naw, it's more than that. That nigga' must be cashing you out or something!"

"Yea he spends money on me. So what if he is? Now who's hating?"

"So? So, cut the nigga' off! It's my turn to cash you out!"

One Week Later

Omies was taking Hillary to get her nails done, when Sasha started calling non-stop, back to back calls. She was even blowing up his phone with texts. *"Answer the phone hoe!!!"* the last message read. Hillary went inside to the nail salon and that was when Omies had a chance to call Sasha back.

"Why the hell you ain't answering your phone, you stupid muthafucka!?" Sasha snapped on him as soon as the call connected.

"Calm the fuck down! Have you lost yo' damn mind or something? What's yo' problem?" he asked her, snapping back.

"You! You my problem! How could you do this to me?" she asked, crying and screaming at the same time.

"What are you talking about?"

"You shady ass bitch! You know what I'm talking about! You have two babies over here muthafucka!" Sasha screamed into the phone.

Misunderstanding her Omies asked, "What? You having, twins?"

"Naw bitch! You got my sister pregnant, you dumb bitch! I hate you!" Sasha screamed through the phone at the top of her lungs. Sasha had already been to his place, trying to kick in the door. Carlos wasn't at home, so she spray painted, "dirty bitch" all over his door.

"Man, I ain't got your sister pregnant, she lying!"

"Bitch, you lying! You gave her $1000 to fuck her and you burnt her! You a dirty muthafucka' and you gonna get yours too, I promise you that!"

He had nothing to say after that. He knew he shouldn't have fucked with her sister. *Bitch couldn't keep her mouth shut and then gonna lie and say I burnt her after I took her ass to the clinic.* "Bae..." was all he could say.

"Bae nothing! You better hope I ain't got shit when I get to the clinic! And be prepared to take care of both these babies, we putting your ass on child support!" then she slammed the phone down.

Omies was in shock. He tried to call back but she didn't answer. *What the fuck?* He thought to himself. He called Carlos up.

"What up?" Carlos answered on the first ring.

"Dog you ain't gonna believe this shit!" Omies said, not wasting any time.

"Man, I already saw it! That shit is fucked up!" Carlos said talking about the spray paint job.

"Saw what? What are you talking about? I'm talking about getting Sasha's sister pregnant and she told Sasha everything," Omies said, wondering what Carlos was talking about.

"I'm talking about someone spray painted "dirty bitch" on the front door. Now it makes sense. It must have been Sasha or her sister, one of the two."

"This bitch talking about ain't neither of them getting an abortion and they putting the friend of the court on me too," Omies told him.

Carlos started laughing, "What?" he laughed again, "What type of shit is that? What the kids gone be brothers and cousins?"

"Man, this shit ain't funny dog! I gotta figure something out quick, they about to try to play me!"

"I don't know what to tell you dog, that's some crazy ass shit! Where you at now?"

"Hold on, Sasha calling me!" He clicked over, "Hello?"

"What's up?" She asked, sounding much calmer, almost like a different person.

"Shit what's up?"

"I got a deal for you?"

"What you mean a deal?"

"Give me $30,000 and we both will get an abortion. If not, fuck you and we'll see you in court!" Sasha said, and then she hung up not even giving him a chance to answer.

Omies clicked back to Carlos who was still on the other line.

"Dog guess what this bitch just said?"

"What?"

"Give her $30,000 and her and Shareal will get an abortion! Thirty G's!" Omies said, shocked at the large number.

"Damn dog! That bitch crazy as hell. How she even know you got that kind of money?" Carlos asked, although he already knew the answer to his own question.

"Man, I don't know, but I'm thinking about just giving it to her, dog. Either that or one of them bitches dead. I can't have two kids that's brothers, or sisters, and cousins. That's some Jerry Springer shit there!" Omies said, laughing at himself a little.

"I feel you dog! But I gotta say if you wasn't out there splurging so damn hard, that bitch wouldn't even come at you like that. That's how she know you got money because you show everyone you got money," Carlos said trying to school him before someone else did the hard way.

Omies was quiet over the phone. He didn't even want to hear that shit Carlos was spitting out his mouth. "Man, I'm about to give that bitch the money and cut all these

dumb ass hoes off except Resa. Fuck these hoes man!"
Omies was fed up.

$30,000 was definitely going to do some damage to his
safe. "Fuck!" he yelled into the phone.

"I'll be at the crib. I'll holla' at you when you get here dog,
be cool man. Don't do nothing stupid!" Carlos advised
him before hanging up.

"Alright," Omies was devastated by the turn of events.
This was turning into one big disaster after another.

Hillary came out smiling after getting her nails done and
painted. "Okay, I'm done, you like?" she asked, flashing
her fingernails in his face. Each nail had his name on it.

"Yeah, that look good." Omies said sounding down.

"What's wrong baby?" Hillary asked, worried about him.
"Nothing. We ain't gonna go shopping today, but here go
a lil cash if you still wanna go." Omies said, putting a wad
of cash into her lap.

"Nooo! I wanted to go with you," she said giving the
money back and pouting in her seat.

"I don't feel too good, I got too much going on right
now."

"You shouldn't mess with so many hoes!" she said to him
as she folded her arms across her chest. It took all of

Omies will power to keep from smacking her ass in her mouth. He was sick to his stomach, and that was no lie. He couldn't believe he got caught up being stupid.

CHAPTER TWENTY-FIVE

R esa answered her phone right away when Kareem called her. "Hey brother!"

"What's up sis'? You called earlier?" Kareem said sounding distracted.

"Yeah, I called you like three times. What you been doing?"

"Nothing, what's up with you

"Um, I got someone for you to get!" Resa said making music for Kareem's ears. He was waiting for that.

"Who?"

"I'm not sure if you know them or not, but my bad if you do... You know them two dudes that stay in your complex? One drive a BMW with rims and the other dude is a Puerto Rican, and drive a Mustang?" Resa asked, describing

"Yeah, I know who you talking about. You know them?"

"Yeah, I know the black dude and Olivia is in love with the other one," Resa explained.

"Shut up! You serious?"

"Yeah, I swear."

"Them nigga's sell dope, don't they? Slim was telling me the other day about them," Kareem told her, remembering how he stopped Slim from robbing them.

"Yeah, I think they do! Whatever they do, they both got money, especially Omies." Resa told him, giving up what could have been a permanent thing for her.

"Omies? Who dat'?"

"That's the black dude name."

"Oh, okay! Well look sis', come see me some time tomorrow so we can set this shit up!"

"Wait, give me a little while. Let me work my way in more and see if it's worth it. I don't want you to take a chance if it's some bullshit."

"Alright, bet! Just let me know when you're ready. I'm like 7 eleven, open 7 days a week, 24 hours a day," Kareem said, making her laugh.

"Okay Kareem, I'll call you when I know something, bye!"

Omies dropped Hillary off at her house and told her he would call her later. Soon as she got out the car, he called Sasha.

"What Omies? You got my money?"

"I wanna see proof that both of y'all is pregnant."

"No problem, you'll get it in the mail in a couple of days," Sasha said, already anticipating him having his doubts.

"Oh, I can't come s..." Sasha hung up on him before he could finish his sentence. He didn't call back but he did call his mom next.

"Hello son," she answered.

"Hey ma, how are you?"

"I'm fine and you?" she asked with other voices in the background.

"I'm ok, can I come and visit you today?"

"Yeah Omies, you know you can come see me anytime."

"I'll swing by later on. I'll see ya later," he said hanging up before she could ask what it was about. His phone was off the chain today. It was ringing like crazy. Fiends were calling him back to back. Omies had to do a lot of running around, but it was worth it in the end. Each fiend served a purpose in his life and spent hundreds of dollars a day, sometimes even a thousand.

Resa had called and wanted him to come get her. He told her he was on his way to see his mother, but he was on his way to pick her up first.

When Resa got in the car, she hugged and gave him a long juicy kiss. "Hey boo!"

"What's up?" He replied, she could tell he wasn't in a good mood. Most of all, she wished she didn't have to go to his moms house with him. Especially debating with herself about setting him up or not. She didn't need no more emotional attachments messing with her head. They drove for about 25 minutes before he arrived at a nice, two story, tan and burgundy house. The house looked brand new.

There was a Jaguar parked in the driveway. His mom was in love with Jaguar and she had been driving them for the last twenty years. They both got out of the car and went up to the door.

"Hey son!" his mom smiled as she gave him a hug, happy to see him. "Who is this pretty girl you have with you?"

CHAPTER TWENTY-SIX

"This is Resa, she is a close friend of mine. Maybe someone I'm thinking of settling down with," he said, looking at Resa with a big smile.

"Oh really?" Resa and his mom both said in unison, causing everyone to laugh.

"Well I guess you must be serious to bring a girl here. I can't remember the last time you did that."

"Resa, this is my mom. You can call her Miss Morry."

They all sat down at the table and relaxed after Miss Morry got everyone something to drink. She was a single woman. She had been single for quite some time now, which was rare for a woman who was only 45 years old but looked 25. She had been in the drug game for almost

27 years. She had it going on and was already probably set for life, but still she played the game.

"So son, what brings you over here out of the blue? I haven't talked to you in months, so it must be something important."

Not sure how to approach the subject Omies said, "I'm in the middle of something crazy right now."

"Something crazy like what?"

Omies just spilled it, he didn't have any more patience to sugar coat it. "I got two kids on the way."

Miss Morry smiled at the thought of having more grand babies. "You having twins?" she asked looking at Resa.

Resa shook her head and didn't speak as she waited for Omies to explain. "I wish. No I have two sisters pregnant!" he said, dropping a bombshell that left Miss Morry speechless and her mouth hanging open.

"Are you serious?" Resa and Miss Morry again spoke in unison.

Resa was just as shocked and didn't understand why Omies would bring her here to hear this. Her and Miss Morry were eyeing each other, and they could see in each other's eyes that this was something new.

"I can't believe you could be so careless. What are you going to do now?"

"I can't have them! I can't deal with either one of them as baby mamas. I'ma get an abortion! But that's gonna cost me $30,000," Omies said telling them the worst of it.

Now Miss Morry knew why he had come. "What? Why $30,000?"

"I don't know, that's the number they asked for."

"See, them those types of little gals you stay away from. They ain't nothing but gold diggers. How you even know you got them pregnant? All I can say is you messed up bad this time. But whatever you gonna do make sure you know you was the one got them pregnant. Get some kind of proof that they even pregnant at all." Miss Morry advised him.

"I slept with them both on the same day, they said they both the same number of weeks pregnant. I can see it being me, but like u said, I need proof," Omies said.

Miss Morry went on and on for hours. She wasn't even sure that Omies had that kind of money. Not with his lavish lifestyle... But if he didn't, it was his problem. That's one thing she didn't help him with, money.

The whole time Resa just sat there listening to them going back and forth, without saying a word. *Wow, he dirty and he expect me to be with him, he must be crazy! Yeah, he fucking with the wrong one* Resa thought to herself.

After saying their goodbyes they were on the way out of the house when Miss Morry called Omies back, while Resa kept walking to the car. "What's up mama?" Omies asked her looking at Resa get inside. He noticed she was real quiet and would probably have a lot to say on the ride home.

"I didn't like that girl. It's something about her. I can't put my finger on it yet but watch her because I think she's fake." Miss Morry warned him about her gut feeling.

"Naw, mama, she cool, she ain't like that. She's a good one and she got a good head on her shoulders."

"Okay, well what you think she thinks about what you just told me?"

CHAPTER TWENTY-SEVEN

"I'm not sure yet, but I'm about to find out by the looks of things," Omies told her as both of them looked at Resa who just stared straight ahead.

"Lord have mercy, Omies watch out for that girl. Listen to me boy." she said as she accepted his kiss on her cheek.

"Okay, I will, I love you, I'll call you when I get the proof," Omies said walking down the walk way and into another ring of fire.

The whole time driving he was thinking about what his mom said. He couldn't figure out what Resa was, but his mama had good intuition about people in general. She seemed to like his presence, but he was going to pay heed to his mom and keep an eye on her.

Resa never questioned him about the babies, in fact she didn't say much at all on that drive home from his mama's house. After he dropped her off he thought he wouldn't hear from her again, but she had been spending a lot of time with him and still found time for Dayshawn as well.

Dayshawn had been calling her, telling her he missed her, so she went to see him. It was about 10:00 p.m. and Resa knew he wanted to fuck. He was a little tipsy off some liquor. When she got to his house he was showing off, counting money on his bed like he was big time. Dayshawn loved showing off, something he and Omies had in common, especially around females, but this time he was showing the wrong one his treasure. As soon as Resa saw all the money, Kareem popped into her head.

"Boy, why you got all that money scattered all over the bed?" she asked smiling.

"I'm counting! You wanna help with the process?"

"Naw, I'm no good at counting money! My talent lies in spending it," she joked.

"Okay well, just give me a few minutes. I'll be done shortly, this only like a hundred thousand, it won't take me long," he bragged.

When Resa heard a hundred thousand, her heart skipped a beat. *Oh, this nigga' hit tonight* she thought to herself.

"I'm gonna make me a drink, you want another one baby?" she went in the kitchen and texted her brother.

He texted her right back that him and Slim were ready for some action. This time their plan was to tie Dayshawn up and torture him until he gave up every penny he had. All Resa could think about was what she was going to do tomorrow with all that money she would receive for her biggest hit ever. It was going down tonight and she was going to fuck and suck the shit out of Dayshawn's dick tonight, and she was going to be happy doing it while keeping him occupied until it was time for her brother to show up. Resa made her way to the bathroom and changed into a sexy lingerie, 3 piece set. Before she went back into the bedroom she unlocked the front door and also unlocked one of the windows just in case Dayshawn happened to check the front door. She then tip toed back into the bedroom to finish getting herself ready for the drama that was about to unfold tonight. Dayshawn was still counting money when she came back into the room... He looked up and saw what she was wearing, an outfit that left very little to the imagination.

"Come here baby! Damn you looking good girl!" he said, pulling her to him with piles of money beneath them as they began stripping each other clothes off. What started as a night of casual sex turned into choking, scratching, biting and wrestling each other into different positions.

They were both excited and horny, each for their own different reasons.

"Fuck this pussy!" Resa screamed at the top of her lungs, as she locked her legs around his back while he was on top of her. She made the best out of rolling around in the money while having this rough and aggressive sex, that is until the door slung open and she seen her brother, and Slim. Resa was happy to see them because she was tired of Dayshawn's little dick, but she was surprised and confused because right behind her brother and Slim were two more guys and they had guns pointed at Slim and Kareem's head. Seconds later, Resa felt a big hard fist hit her mouth, hard enough that it busted both of her lips open. Dayshawn then hit her in the eye with his other fist, closing it right up. All Resa could do was cover up into a ball and scream.

Kareem was standing there, too helpless to do anything for his sister. The two big guys and Dayshawn began tying Resa, Kareem, and Slim's mouth's, hands, and feet with duct tape. Then they sat them down in the corner. No one said nothing. They seemed to be waiting for someone else. Gage and then Miss Morry soon walked in right behind them. Gage had a baby tiger on the side of him on a thick chained leash. Resa was very surprised to see Miss Morry.

Since the last robbery, Dayshawn had paid for some surveillance cameras to be set up around the house and he had Gage next door watching everything. Dayshawn and Gage were neighbors and Gage had been suspecting Kareem ever since he was robbed . Once he figured out that Resa and Kareem were brother and sister, it wasn't too hard to put two and two together. The first thing Gage did was call Omies mom, Miss Morry, to see if she knew anything about Kareem or Resa. Since she had just met Resa she wanted to get involved in case her son was a target as well.

Miss Morry and Gage went way back, they both were old school legends in the area.

Miss Morry ripped the tape from Resa's mouth, making Resa feel like her lips were getting torn off. It hurt even more because her lips were busted open, raw and bleeding. "Owww!" she yelled out in pain.

"Do I know you little girl?" Miss Morry asked her.

Resa was afraid to say anything other than, "We've met."

"What were you doing with my son? Was you planning on robbing him too?" the room was silent as Miss Morry asked the questions. No one dared to interrupt her.

"N..N..No, I like Omies, he's sweet to me. He's someone I can see myself with," Resa said hoping his mom would have mercy on her.

"Well then, why you over in the bed with this one if you so down with my boy?"

"I...I..." Resa was stuttering. She knew she had gotten herself in some deep shit but she had no idea how deep, she figured she had a good chance to get out of this mess still.

Kareem looked like he was trying to say something so Gage ripped the tape of his mouth. "What? What you got to say?"

CHAPTER TWENTY-EIGHT

"It was all me. I followed my sister over here. She had nothing to do with any of it," Kareem said trying to save his sisters life. Resa began to feel a little better about her situation knowing her brother had her back. "She didn't know I was following her, she had nothing to do with it. Just let her go and take me," Kareem said gallantly taking the fall.

Gage nodded his head like he appreciated Kareem stepping up like a man, then he slowly reached into his pocket and pulled out a DVD and slipped it into the player, he picked up the remote from the dresser and fast forwarded the DVD to the part where Resa was tip toeing her way as she unlocked the front door and then the window, then she went back into the bathroom. Gage shut off the TV and secured the tape back on Kareem's mouth. "Trick no good son!"

Miss Morry was still talking to Resa, and so far, there was nothing Resa was telling her that had her convinced that she wasn't going to set her son up as well. Resa was a snake and now it was time to pay the price. Miss Morry reached into her purse and pulled out a cherry bomb firework, the kind with the long green wick. She was debating in her mind whether to put the cherry bomb in Resa's mouth or inside her pussy. She was already naked. Miss Morry shoved a rag into her mouth and then a fresh piece of duct tape held the rag in place. Then she had Dayshawn and one of the other men hold Resa's legs in the air and apart while she jammed the cherry bomb inside Resa's pussy. It slipped in and began to sink a little so Miss Morry had to be fast to grab the wick before the bomb disappeared all the way in.

Grabbing a lighter from the guy that was still holding Slim and Kareem at gunpoint, Miss Morry went to light the fuse as Resa tried to back away, but Miss Morry had already lit it. Dayshawn, the other guy and Miss Morry all backed away and four seconds later all you heard was a "Blop!!" sound.

Resa's eyes were permanently stuck wide open. And the firework had killed her as it exploded inside her organs.

Blood, guts and intestines began to seep out of where her pussy used to be. Her asshole and pussy had become one giant sinkhole. The fluids were uncontrollable and unstoppable and the smell was horrible.

Kareem threw up and chunks leaked out the side of his tape. His eyes watered from tears and coughing as he begin choking on his own vomit. He couldn't even look in her direction.

Miss Morry smiled at her work, she had always wanted to do that.

Gage ripped the tape off Kareem's mouth and the left over vomit spilled to the floor as he coughed up the rest. "What should I do with you Kareem? I trusted you and Slim. I gave you two a living and you got greedy. What you thought a old school guy like me couldn't get the muscle up to pay you back or did you think I was too stupid to recognize that stupid ass grill?" Gage asked him as he aimed his gun barrel against his forehead. Kareem was silent as tears slipped down his cheeks. He had just watched his sister die a horrible death. Nothing they could do to him would ever measure up to the pain he had just felt, so he thought.

"Don't cry now tough guy! You like taking from people, face the consequences like a man instead of a bitch! What the hell was you two thinking when you took my 2 kilos of cocaine? Did you honestly think I was going to let that go? Man I've been doing business in that park for years and nothing like that has ever happened to me. All I really have to say to you my man is you fucked with the wrong one!" Gage was trying to hold his tiger back from Resa's dead corpse the whole time he was talking but he gave up and let it feast on Resa's body. The tiger lunged at her and tossed her until he got his fill. When the tiger was done he lay over what was left of Resa, licking his chops as he eyed his next possible prey, Slim and Kareem. Resa had so many chunks bit out of her, she looked like a giant puzzle piece with parts of her missing from every limb and torso.

Kareem could only stare at his sister and imagine what she used to look like.

"Get these muthafuckas' up," Gage told the other two men. They helped Kareem and Slim to their feet and carried them into Dayshawn's garage, where an all-black, sparkly van was waiting. Kareem and Slim were thrown in the back of the van and Gage made Kareem tell them where he lived. Kareem shook his head no and Gage pulled the tiger up and let the tiger nibble on Kareem's fingers like they were appetizers from a restaurant. The tiger had bit the tip of two fingers so far and Kareem was screaming through the tape. When he finally gave up the address, they drove to his place. On the way to Kareem's apartment, Gage noticed Carlos and a Resa look alike walking towards him. He knew Resa had a twin, but he had not found a shred of proof linking Olivia to the scheme, so he just greeted her and kept walking by. After searching through the apartment, it didn't take Gage long to find what he was looking for. Kareem and Slim were not too imaginative when it came to hiding places. Fifteen minutes later, Gage exited their apartment with a duffel bag filled with money and dope inside. He had got most of his dope back and more money than he had lost, plus some guns.

When he got to the parking lot, Miss Morry was waiting in her silver Jaguar. She popped the trunk from inside the car and Gage threw the bag inside and then jumped back into the van.

Gage held is tiger as he wanted more of Kareem flesh. Even as a baby, you could see the muscles beneath the black stripes each time the tiger moved. Josh, the other hit man, kept driving, making sure to stay within the speed limit. Slim could see the pain that Kareem was in and he could only imagine what was in store for him because as of yet, nothing had happened to him. They drove for hours, with Kareem and Slim nodding off only to be awakened each time the tiger roared. They finally arrived at a farm in the middle of nowhere that Gage owned. The nearest neighbor was ten miles away. The farm had chickens, pigs and horses that he took care of. Josh drove the van into the barn and they all got out, being careful to keep their guns on Slim and Kareem. They cut the tape from their legs so they didn't have to carry them any longer. Kareem's mind was going crazy, blood was still seeping from his chewed off fingers and he knew he was going to die, but HOW was the question? He was also beginning to wonder why they hadn't hurt Slim yet.

As they walked in the direction they were ordered he gave Slim the evil eye and Slim just shrugged his shoulders like he didn't know a thing. *This muthafucka' is a phony! Why the hell haven't they done anything to him yet,* Kareem thought to himself. Slim was scared to death at what was going to happen next, but he was wondering if his luck was going to hold out since they hadn't done anything to him, he had yet to feel any pain.

Why the hell does Kareem keep looking at me? Does he have a plan to get away or what? I hope he don't think I'm with any of these crazy fuckers. I would never betray him, we here together, we die together.

CHAPTER TWENTY-NINE

They were taken to a room inside the farm with two mattresses, twin size, about 10 feet apart from each other. Attached to the beds were straps for a person's hands and feet. But what was strange was the 2 horses that were suspended in the air, with their dicks sticking straight out. Gage had shot them full of the animal version of Viagra hours ago, plus a dose of speed.

Kareem and Slim didn't know what to make of this operation. Gage walked up behind them and injected them with something in their necks. Kareem felt light headed and he saw Slim pass out from the drug and then he felt himself falling.

When they woke up, they were completely naked, with the horse's dicks in their asses, ripping their assholes apart. The horse fucked them for hours, until their bodies could no longer take the pain of the horse's dicks ripping their insides apart.

Four hours later, they were dead, and still the horse humped their limp bodies until they were exhausted.

The Next Day

Omies and Carlos left Sasha's place after dropping off the $30,000 in cash when Carlos received a call from Olivia, she was crying her heart out about her brother and sister.

Their bodies had been found inside numerous garbage bags on her mother's front porch. It was all over the news.

Carlos couldn't believe what he was hearing, but he did his best to calm her down, although she was inconsolable.

Omies had rented an orange and black Dodge Charger to continue with his business. He had just left the post office with their weekly delivery and was on his way back home when he heard a police siren go off, "Whoop, whoop!"

"Aww shit!" Omies said, getting a bad feeling in his gut.

"Just chill out man! They ain't got no reason to search us, just play it cool," Carlos told him, praying he was right.

Omies didn't want to pull over, but he took the chance that it was for some minor traffic infraction. He was nervous and began to get a sweat trail down his forehead.

"License and registration please," the officer said.

"What's the problem officer? I wasn't speeding was I?" Omies asked, as he saw 4, unmarked police cars driving up. "Man, what the fuck!" he whispered to Carlos.

"Dog, mash it! They on to us, that's the FEDS right there!" Carlos pointed out, as men got out of their unmarked cars, with assault rifles drawn and DEA stamped on their bullet proof vests.

Omies dropped the Charger into drive and sped off, burning rubber and weaving his way through the police cars that were trying to barricade them in. Dayshawn was right, the feds were on to them. They had just picked up a kilo of cocaine from the post office and they were being watched doing it.

Omies sped through town, running red lights, trying to get away until he saw the helicopter above, then he knew it was pointless.

"Fuck man, we gotta stop dog! It's a wrap, we ain't getting away from that muthafucka' up there," Omies said pointing to the sky. "Fuck it dog!" he said as he started to pull over and put the car in park.

The police swarmed around them with their guns drawn. "PUT YOUR FUCKING HANDS UP! NOW!" the police ordered them through a loud speaker. "Hands on the steering wheel and don't move assholes!" another voice yelled out. A dozen DEA agents converged on the Charger and pulled them out one by one, daring them to make a move.

While they were being handcuffed, the federal agent in charge came up to them, "You're under arrest. Anything you say can and will be used against you in a court of law," he said, giving them their Miranda rights.

That was all Omies remembered until he woke up the next morning in a federal holding cell. "Hey, can I get a toothbrush and some toothpaste?" he yelled out, trying to get the guards attention.

"Yeah, but first you have a visitor that wants to see you," a burly, white, bald headed guard said as he pulled out his key to open the door.

"Who is it?" Omies asked, as he put his hands out to be handcuffed.

"You'll see," the guard said as he practically pushed him down the hall to a small, visiting room. Two men, in suits were waiting for him to enter.

"Hi Mr. Morry, I'm agent Saye," the older of the two agents said as he came in. They motioned for him to sit down.

"I'm agent Ford," the other, younger and better dressed agent said.

"And?" Omies asked, with attitude. The two detectives laughed and shut the door.

"You must not know how serious this is?" Agent Ford said, smiling at him. Omies was silent, not willing to give them the satisfaction, as he sat hunched over.

"Carlos already told us how everything works with you guys. He told us that you guys receive a kilo of cocaine every week," Detective Ford said, still smiling at Omies arrogant attitude.

"Fuck you and Carlos!" Omies told him, staring him down.

Agent Saye snapped and pushed Omies hard against the wall. "Look you piece of shit! You think we're blind? You little fucker! We know all about you, you pussy!" he then grabbed him by his neck, squeezing harder with each word. "You're going down asshole!"

Omies started choking and still he smiled at them. He didn't believe the shit they was saying, he wasn't falling for their games. He knew he was facing some years for the kilo, but he had to suck it up.

Later on, he found out Carlos was still in the jail and not talking. Not that he gave a damn because he wasn't going to say a word. They had tried the same thing on Carlos, saying Omies had turned, but Carlos didn't fall for it.

They both went to court together and got arraigned.

They were debating on who was going to take the primary charge. They were both going to get charged for the same thing and their bond was $100,000 each. Whoever coped to the main charge could get the sentence, leaving the other to walk free or they could both go down together for it, giving them both a sentence.

Carlos had already spoken to the bail bondsman and he was ready to come get him out, Olivia was all over it for her man. But Omies, his cash wasn't right at all. He had been blowing so much money lately he couldn't afford to bail himself out nor afford to buy himself a good lawyer. He was too ashamed to ask Carlos for the money, so he figured he would sit in jail a couple of months, until he sold a few things.

Once they got inside the court room, Omies and Carlos were busy whispering back and forth.

"Hey man, don't even trip dog. Go out there and take care of your son. I'ma take the charge and lay down, you just be careful out there dog," Omies whispered.

Carlos's stomach dropped to the floor when he heard that. His eyes started watering up and turning red, it took every muscle in his body not to cry. He was speechless. He never thought Omies would do something so unselfish. All he could do was dap his boy. Omies wasn't going to let the feds fuck them both over. So he figured he'd set Carlos free and hopefully Carlos would ride with him through it.

Carlos was able to bond out hours later, but he had to be on a tether until everything was settled with the case.

Omies and Hillary became closer and closer. She took care of everything he owned and was owed. After Omies wrote the prosecutor saying that Carlos had nothing to do with the drugs or high speed chase, Carlos's charges were dismissed and Omie's bond was raised even higher. Hillary had got him a real good lawyer, who said he would be able to have Omies out in 5 years on tether at most. He was charging her $70,000 to make it happen. But Hillary made sure he received every penny through making consistent payments.

She made her way to visit Omies twice a week and she put $100 a week in his account to spend on commissary,.

Carlos continued to do his thing and mess with Olivia.

He and his baby mama were able to work out a deal. As long as he gave her $200 a week, plus did things for the baby, he could come see him anytime. He hated her for it, but he sucked it up, because he didn't want to deal with the courts.

Months later, Omies was sentenced to 5 years in a federal penitentiary and 3 years on tether afterwards. Hillary was there 100% for him, and Carlos was as well.

A couple of weeks later, after Sasha and Shareal had their abortions, their bodies were found inside the trunk of a brand new Jaguar in a dealership car lot.

Omies watched it being played all over the news, smiling to himself. *"I love you mom,"* he said to himself.

OTHER BOOKS BY THE AUTHOR

Women Lie Men Lie part 1

Women Lie Men Lie part 2

Women Lie Men Lie part 3

Naive To The Streets

Girls Fall Like Dominoes

Please, please please, leave a review.

https://www.amazon.com/A-Roy-Milligan/e/B009YEVZPC?
ref=sr_ntt_srch_lnk_2&qid=1587560927&sr=8-2

NEW RELEASES

SOSA GANG 2 by ROMELL TUKES

KINGZ OF THE GAME 7 by PLAYA RAY

SKI MASK MONEY 2 by RENTA

BORN IN THE GRAVE 3 by SELF MADE TAY

NIGHTMARE ON SILENT AVE II

THE PLUG OF LIL MEXICO II

By **Chris Green**

THE STREETS WILL TALK II

By **Yolanda Moore**

SON OF A DOPE FIEND III

HEAVEN GOT A GHETTO III

SKI MASK MONEY III

By **Renta**

LOYALTY AIN'T PROMISED III

By **Keith Williams**

ANGEL V

By **Anthony Fields**

THE STREETS WILL NEVER CLOSE IV

By **K'ajji**

HARD AND RUTHLESS III

KILLA KOUNTY IV

By **Khufu**

MONEY GAME III

By **Smoove Dolla**

COKE GIRLZ II

COKE BOYS II

CHI'RAQ GANGSTAS V

SOSA GANG III

BRONX SAVAGES II

BODYMORE KINGPINS II

By **Romell Tukes**

Playa Ray
HERE TODAY GONE TOMORROW II
By Fly Rock
REAL G'S MOVE IN SILENCE II
By Von Diesel
GRIMEY WAYS IV
By Ray Vinci

Available Now

RESTRAINING ORDER **I & II**
By **CA$H & Coffee**
LOVE KNOWS NO BOUNDARIES **I II & III**
By **Coffee**
RAISED AS A GOON I, II, III & IV
BRED BY THE SLUMS I, II, III
BLAST FOR ME I & II
ROTTEN TO THE CORE I II III
A BRONX TALE I, II, III
DUFFLE BAG CARTEL I II III IV V VI
HEARTLESS GOON I II III IV V
A SAVAGE DOPEBOY I II
DRUG LORDS I II III
CUTTHROAT MAFIA I II

KING OF THE TRENCHES

By **Ghost**

LAY IT DOWN **I & II**

LAST OF A DYING BREED I II

BLOOD STAINS OF A SHOTTA I & II III

By **Jamaica**

LOYAL TO THE GAME I II III

LIFE OF SIN I, II III

By **TJ & Jelissa**

BLOODY COMMAS I & II

SKI MASK CARTEL I II & III

KING OF NEW YORK I II,III IV V

RISE TO POWER I II III

COKE KINGS I II III IV V

BORN HEARTLESS I II III IV

KING OF THE TRAP I II

By **T.J. Edwards**

IF LOVING HIM IS WRONG…I & II

LOVE ME EVEN WHEN IT HURTS I II III

By **Jelissa**

WHEN THE STREETS CLAP BACK I & II III

THE HEART OF A SAVAGE I II III IV

MONEY MAFIA I II

LOYAL TO THE SOIL I II III

By **Jibril Williams**

A DISTINGUISHED THUG STOLE MY HEART I II & III

LOVE SHOULDN'T HURT I II III IV

RENEGADE BOYS I II III IV

PAID IN KARMA I II III

SAVAGE STORMS I II III

AN UNFORESEEN LOVE I II III

BABY, I'M WINTERTIME COLD I II

By **Meesha**

A GANGSTER'S CODE I &, II III

A GANGSTER'S SYN I II III

THE SAVAGE LIFE I II III

CHAINED TO THE STREETS I II III

BLOOD ON THE MONEY I II III

A GANGSTA'S PAIN I II III

By J-Blunt

PUSH IT TO THE LIMIT

By **Bre' Hayes**

BLOOD OF A BOSS **I, II, III, IV, V**

SHADOWS OF THE GAME

TRAP BASTARD

By **Askari**

THE STREETS BLEED MURDER **I, II & III**

THE HEART OF A GANGSTA I II& III

By **Jerry Jackson**

CUM FOR ME I II III IV V VI VII VIII

An **LDP Erotica Collaboration**

BRIDE OF A HUSTLA **I II & II**

THE FETTI GIRLS **I, II& III**

CORRUPTED BY A GANGSTA I, II III, IV

BLINDED BY HIS LOVE

THE PRICE YOU PAY FOR LOVE I, II ,III

DOPE GIRL MAGIC I II III

By **Destiny Skai**

WHEN A GOOD GIRL GOES BAD

By **Adrienne**

THE COST OF LOYALTY I II III

By Kweli

A GANGSTER'S REVENGE **I II III & IV**

THE BOSS MAN'S DAUGHTERS I II III IV V

A SAVAGE LOVE **I & II**

BAE BELONGS TO ME I II

A HUSTLER'S DECEIT I, II, III

WHAT BAD BITCHES DO I, II, III

SOUL OF A MONSTER I II III

KILL ZONE

A DOPE BOY'S QUEEN I II III

TIL DEATH

By **Aryanna**

A KINGPIN'S AMBITON

A KINGPIN'S AMBITION **II**

I MURDER FOR THE DOUGH

By **Ambitious**

TRUE SAVAGE I II III IV V VI VII

DOPE BOY MAGIC I, II, III

MIDNIGHT CARTEL I II III

CITY OF KINGZ I II

NIGHTMARE ON SILENT AVE

THE PLUG OF LIL MEXICO II

CLASSIC CITY

By **Chris Green**

A DOPEBOY'S PRAYER

By **Eddie "Wolf" Lee**

THE KING CARTEL **I, II & III**

By **Frank Gresham**

THESE NIGGAS AIN'T LOYAL **I, II & III**

By **Nikki Tee**

GANGSTA SHYT **I II &III**

By **CATO**

THE ULTIMATE BETRAYAL

By **Phoenix**

BOSS'N UP **I , II & III**

By **Royal Nicole**

I LOVE YOU TO DEATH

By **Destiny J**

I RIDE FOR MY HITTA

I STILL RIDE FOR MY HITTA

By **Misty Holt**

LOVE & CHASIN' PAPER

By **Qay Crockett**

TO DIE IN VAIN

SINS OF A HUSTLA

By **ASAD**

BROOKLYN HUSTLAZ

By **Boogsy Morina**

BROOKLYN ON LOCK I & II

By **Sonovia**

GANGSTA CITY

By **Teddy Duke**

A DRUG KING AND HIS DIAMOND I & II III

A DOPEMAN'S RICHES

HER MAN, MINE'S TOO I, II

CASH MONEY HO'S

THE WIFEY I USED TO BE I II

PRETTY GIRLS DO NASTY THINGS

By Nicole Goosby

TRAPHOUSE KING **I II & III**

KINGPIN KILLAZ I II III

STREET KINGS I II

PAID IN BLOOD **I II**

CARTEL KILLAZ I II III

DOPE GODS I II

By **Hood Rich**

LIPSTICK KILLAH **I, II, III**

CRIME OF PASSION I II & III

FRIEND OR FOE I II III

By **Mimi**

STEADY MOBBN' **I, II, III**

THE STREETS STAINED MY SOUL I II III

By **Marcellus Allen**

WHO SHOT YA **I, II, III**

SON OF A DOPE FIEND I II

HEAVEN GOT A GHETTO I II

SKI MASK MONEY I II

Renta

GORILLAZ IN THE BAY **I II III IV**

TEARS OF A GANGSTA I II

3X KRAZY I II

STRAIGHT BEAST MODE I II

DE'KARI

TRIGGADALE I II III

MURDAROBER WAS THE CASE I II

Elijah R. Freeman

GOD BLESS THE TRAPPERS I, II, III

THESE SCANDALOUS STREETS I, II, III

FEAR MY GANGSTA I, II, III IV, V

THESE STREETS DON'T LOVE NOBODY I, II

BURY ME A G I, II, III, IV, V

A GANGSTA'S EMPIRE I, II, III, IV

THE DOPEMAN'S BODYGAURD I II

THE REALEST KILLAZ I II III

THE LAST OF THE OGS I II III

Tranay Adams

THE STREETS ARE CALLING

Duquie Wilson

MARRIED TO A BOSS I II III

By Destiny Skai & Chris Green

KINGZ OF THE GAME I II III IV V VI VII

CRIME BOSS

Playa Ray

SLAUGHTER GANG I II III

RUTHLESS HEART I II III

By Willie Slaughter

FUK SHYT

By Blakk Diamond

DON'T F#CK WITH MY HEART I II

By Linnea

ADDICTED TO THE DRAMA I II III

IN THE ARM OF HIS BOSS II

By Jamila

YAYO I II III IV

A SHOOTER'S AMBITION I II

BRED IN THE GAME

By S. Allen

TRAP GOD I II III

RICH $AVAGE I II III

MONEY IN THE GRAVE I II III

By Martell Troublesome Bolden

FOREVER GANGSTA I II

GLOCKS ON SATIN SHEETS I II

By Adrian Dulan

TOE TAGZ I II III IV

LEVELS TO THIS SHYT I II

IT'S JUST ME AND YOU

By Ah'Million

KINGPIN DREAMS I II III

RAN OFF ON DA PLUG

By Paper Boi Rari

CONFESSIONS OF A GANGSTA I II III IV

CONFESSIONS OF A JACKBOY I II

By Nicholas Lock

I'M NOTHING WITHOUT HIS LOVE

SINS OF A THUG

TO THE THUG I LOVED BEFORE

A GANGSTA SAVED XMAS

IN A HUSTLER I TRUST

By Monet Dragun

CAUGHT UP IN THE LIFE I II III

THE STREETS NEVER LET GO I II III

KHADIFI

IF YOU CROSS ME ONCE I II

ANGEL I II III IV

IN THE BLINK OF AN EYE

By **Anthony Fields**

THE LIFE OF A HOOD STAR

By **Ca$h & Rashia Wilson**

THE STREETS WILL NEVER CLOSE I II III

By **K'ajji**

CREAM I II III

THE STREETS WILL TALK

By **Yolanda Moore**

NIGHTMARES OF A HUSTLA I II III

By **King Dream**

CONCRETE KILLA I II III

VICIOUS LOYALTY I II III

By **Kingpen**

HARD AND RUTHLESS I II

MOB TOWN 251

THE BILLIONAIRE BENTLEYS I II III

REAL G'S MOVE IN SILENCE

By **Von Diesel**

GHOST MOB

Stilloan Robinson

MOB TIES I II III IV V VI

SOUL OF A HUSTLER, HEART OF A KILLER I II

GORILLAZ IN THE TRENCHES

By **SayNoMore**

BODYMORE MURDERLAND I II III

THE BIRTH OF A GANGSTER I II

By Delmont Player

FOR THE LOVE OF A BOSS

By C. D. Blue

MOBBED UP I II III IV

THE BRICK MAN I II III IV V

THE COCAINE PRINCESS I II III IV V VI VII

By King Rio

KILLA KOUNTY I II III IV

By Khufu

MONEY GAME I II

By Smoove Dolla

A GANGSTA'S KARMA I II III

By FLAME

KING OF THE TRENCHES I II III

by **GHOST & TRANAY ADAMS**

QUEEN OF THE ZOO I II

By Black Migo

GRIMEY WAYS I II III

By Ray Vinci

XMAS WITH AN ATL SHOOTER

By Ca$h & Destiny Skai

KING KILLA

By Vincent "Vitto" Holloway

BETRAYAL OF A THUG I II

By Fre$h

THE MURDER QUEENS I II

By Michael Gallon

TREAL LOVE

BOOKS BY LDP'S CEO, CA$H

TRUST IN NO MAN

TRUST IN NO MAN 2

TRUST IN NO MAN 3

BONDED BY BLOOD

SHORTY GOT A THUG

THUGS CRY

THUGS CRY 2

THUGS CRY 3

TRUST NO BITCH

TRUST NO BITCH 2

TRUST NO BITCH 3

TIL MY CASKET DROPS

RESTRAINING ORDER

RESTRAINING ORDER 2

IN LOVE WITH A CONVICT

LIFE OF A HOOD STAR

XMAS WITH AN ATL SHOOTER

www.ingramcontent.com/pod-product-compliance
Lightning Source LLC
Chambersburg PA
CBHW071203260626
47162CB00003B/1147